The Enemy's Kiss

ZANDRIA MUNSON

First published in Great Britain 2012
by Mills & Boon,
an imprint of Harlequin (UK) Limited,
Large Print edition 2012
Harlequin (UK) Limited, Eton House,
18-24 Paradise Road, Richmond, Surrey TW9 1SR

ISBN: 978 0 263 23042 0

Harlequin (UK) policy is to use papers that are natural, renewable and recyclable products and made from wood grown in sustainable forests. The logging and manufacturing process conform to the legal environmental regulations of the country of origin.

Printed and bound in Great Britain
by CPI Antony Rowe, Chippenham, Wiltshire

Dear Reader

The Enemy's Kiss is the continuation of a romantic saga that follows the Drakon clan. My passion for these dark guardians of the night—gargoyles—has compelled me to dig deeper into the complex and intoxicating lives of the Drakon brothers.

Not too dissimilar from my first book for Nocturne that featured one of the Drakon brothers, *Heiress to a Curse*, I found my inspiration for this romance in dark and ancient places. Of late I have been visiting an old convent that is seemingly nestled away from civilization. With its lonely gardens and stone sculptures, it is the perfect location to allow one's mind to wander far beyond mundane things.

I also found that such a place would make an excellent backdrop for a scene in this novel, and thus incorporated a monastery into it. I trust you will find Nicholas and Daniela's story as spellbinding as the first.

Enjoy!

For my adorable little mother, Martha.

Prologue

Romania, 1820

Fire raged throughout the city of Cetatea. The flames rose to scorch the midnight sky and choke the stars with its thick and blackened smoke. Nicholas Drakon stood on the rise that overlooked the large and once prosperous city. Shame enveloped him as he absorbed the cries of the innocent that were subdued only by the victorious shrieks of his clansmen; those who had gone against the principles set forth by Nicholas's father, Lord Victor, leader of the Drakon clan.

Things hadn't always been this way. There'd been a time of unity and peace, but that was long before they were all afflicted by the dreadful curse. The decades had passed and the rift within his clan had swelled, resulting in an outrageous battle of wills and the deaths of many innocents. Too long had these wayward members been allowed to proceed with mere warning and chastisement. The time had come to put an end to it.

Nicholas flexed his grip on the large sword he held. Over his shoulder he cast the thirteen warriors he led a look that warned them to be prepared. With the forms of hulking men and the faces of beasts, they were ready for the inevitable battle that lay ahead, dressed in heavy, intricately worked silver breastplates and bracers of matching quality encasing their wrists. They were slaves and lords of the darkness. Stone by day and gargoyle by night, they'd once been men, but were now damned for eternity.

At his back, Nicholas flexed great and taloned

wings, ready for flight. From the hilltop adjacent to the one upon which he stood, his brothers Simion and Marius observed the holocaust. Simion raised a torch, signaling the commencement of the attack. Steel in his grip, Nicholas and his warriors took to the skies. Their mission was to capture as many of their own alive, but much blood would be spilled this night, he knew. His heart ached for the many who would fall dead by his hands, but this was no time for weakness. What had to be done must be done.

Fagara Castle, later

The vicious cries could be felt throughout the castle. They shook the walls and coursed through the stone floors. Nicholas, along with his father and brothers marched down the steps that lead to the dungeon entrance.

Chained to the walls were the remaining twelve defectors. Among them was the one called Gabriel. Once a man of honor and integrity, he'd become consumed by rage as the

Drakon clan had been forced to abandon much of their lands and holdings. They'd been driven deeper into the forest to avoid being hunted by those who deemed their kind an abomination. His fury had swelled even more as Lord Victor had simply accepted this fate, choosing peace over violence. Gabriel had thus formed his own alliance with the intent to destroy any who threatened their family. He'd in turn become the greatest opposition of the Drakon clan; what was worse, he was the younger brother of Lord Victor.

Lord Victor moved to face his brother. With his massive wings beating against the damp air, Gabriel fought against the chains that bound him. But it was to no avail, for the chains, made from an alloy called titanium, had been purposefully fashioned for this function.

"Ah, brother," Gabriel said with a venomous sneer. "I suspect you are pleased with yourself for slaughtering so many of your own."

Lord Victor's head fell a measure. "About as

pleased as I am for what I am forced to do this night. I can no longer stand by and allow you to wreak havoc."

Gabriel erupted in a loud, derisive laugh. "You speak as if I am at fault. Nay, brother. It is you who brought this curse upon us all." He sobered, his eyes hard as he continued. "You and your lust for peasant flesh."

Nicholas's eyes narrowed upon his uncle as he steeled himself to remain as he was. It was no secret that the gargoyle curse had been brewed in a single night of lies and deception. Their mother had been a simple peasant girl when she'd captured Lord Victor's heart, driving him to abandon a senseless betrothal. In a fit of rage, his wealthy and greedy intended bride, Lady Vivian, had spun a web of lies to her cousin Necesar, a powerful sorceress. Vivian had pleaded for vengeance, but even that hadn't been enough to remedy her discontent. Anger had compelled her to a point of insanity, and in one final act of rage she'd torched her family's castle, taking not only her own life but those of all who dwelled there.

And so, armed with the notion that Lord Victor had not only severed the betrothal after forcing himself on her cousin, but that he was also the one to be blamed for Vivian's death, Necesar concocted a fierce spell, cursing the Drakon bloodline for all eternity.

Lord Victor looked weary. "No man should be made to suffer for the choices of his heart."

"Aye," Gabriel spat. "Just as an entire clan should not be punished for their leader's irresponsible follies."

Lord Drakon turned away then, his eyes solemn as he fastened a look upon the figure of a hunched and ageless woman who before had gone unnoticed. She advanced, her weathered face coming to rest upon Gabriel. She was called Agatha, and was a witch of the Ananovian clan. Dwellers of the hills of eastern Romania, this secluded race of witches had lent their assistance to the gargoyles for decades in return for protection. They were healers, not fighters, but their abilities were matched by none.

Agatha reached within her cloak and pulled forth two palm-sized flat, circular stones with hollowed centers. She kneeled, placing each onto the floor before her. Engraved with the sacred symbols of the Ananovian witch clan, they were called the Runes of Moloch and Cythe. They'd been harvested from the bowels of the earth and animated by the most powerful Ananovian warlocks. They were used in binding spells to contain spirits or souls of those who required captivity.

Before them, Gabriel wrenched at the chains, shaking the room once again with another fierce growl. "Sorcery! I see you have reached a new low, Victor!" he spat.

Lord Victor said nothing. He stepped back as the witch began to chant. A serpent-like stream of smoke crawled from beneath her cloak, swelling into a translucent cloud that quickly spun a web about the gargoyles who were fastened to the walls. They began to shriek and rip at the chains that bound them as the cold transformation to granite crept up their legs, snaking through their veins and freezing everything in its wake.

"Until we meet again, brother," Gabriel spoke. A moment later he'd become a solid mass of stone.

Agatha retrieved the runes from the floor and handed them to Lord Victor. A veil of grief fell over his face before he accepted them.

"These runes bind their souls now," Agatha spoke. "Destroy the stones and you will release your brother and his followers. They must be secured."

Nicholas's gaze strayed over the twelve statues, each frozen in a pose of rage and anguish. There was no question as to whether his father's judgment had been deserved, for countless efforts had been made to reform the wayward gargoyles. Whether his father would choose to make it an eternal sentence, he didn't know. Whether the world would ever be ready for Gabriel's release was an even greater speculation.

Chapter 1

New York, present day

This was going to be easier than taking candy from a baby.

Daniela Ferreira adjusted the focus on her high-powered night-vision binoculars. She stood on the roof of the five-story building opposite the Langara gallery. From her vantage point, she could see directly into the wide glass windows that lined the front of the establishment. It was nearing 10:00 p.m and the owners were still busy unpacking crates of antiques. She had intended to hit a jewelry store tonight as well, but this was more important. Just within the walls of the gallery lay the item called the Rune of Moloch. It was said to be hundreds of years old and worth a hefty sum. From the illustrations she'd been given, it looked like nothing more than a flat rock. But then she never questioned a buyer's interest in a particular item. She was hired to steal and deliver, and as long as she got paid for the task, she couldn't care less about motives.

Stealing was a way of life for Daniela. It was her profession; a necessity for survival after her mother had walked out on her and her younger sister. Daniela had only been seventeen at the time. Ever since then she'd made a living robbing others. Her missions had gotten bigger and her equipment more advanced, but one thing hadn't changed: she was still a thief.

Turning the knob on the top of the binoculars, she zoomed in on the two men who were still busy inside the gallery. They had removed their blazers and rolled up their shirtsleeves, and she could see the distinct outline of thick, corded muscles flexing beneath their shirts.

She'd heard of this pair; the Drakon brothers. They were renowned for their great business success and their incredible good looks. It seemed that the rumors served them justice. Tall and swarthy, they resembled the heroes of ancient Rome. Even from this distance their dark, chiseled features were unmistakable.

Lowering the device, she unsnapped the collar of her black leather catsuit—it was getting quite warm in the skintight attire. To distract herself, she reset the timer on her wristwatch. She'd done her research and knew full well that an advanced security system had been installed. Once inside the building, she'd have approximately five minutes to locate the Rune of Moloch, steal it and get the hell out of there before the police arrived.

When Daniela looked through the binoculars again, she noticed that a black Rolls Royce had pulled in front of the establishment. The driver held the door open as a woman exited. The woman moved carefully up the stone stairs in front of the building, no doubt hindered by the weight of her protruding abdomen.

Daniela's mouth contorted with a wavering hint of jealousy. She briefly wondered if she'd ever find herself in such a state—pregnant and in a dress. At this rate, such a possibility seemed nonexistent. She was twenty-five and still a virgin.

Between conducting burglaries, evading the authorities and raising her sister, she simply had no time for men and their very expectant personalities. At least that's what she told herself. Deep down inside she knew that she craved companionship.

She forced the thoughts from her mind and focused on the scene playing before her. The woman had entered the building and was immediately pulled into the embrace of one of the Drakon brothers. He placed an affectionate kiss on her lips before checking his watch.

Daniela couldn't suppress the smile that crawled to her lips when he retrieved his blazer from the top of an unpacked crate and slipped it on.

She twisted her long, curly hair into a bun at her nape and pulled her black latex mask on. "Showtime."

Nicholas Drakon pressed down on the crowbar until the lid of the small wooden crate creaked open. This was the last of them. The entire shipment had come from Romania and had arrived on schedule. The delivery consisted of twenty pieces from England, China and Spain, all dating back to the early 1500s.

He and his brother Marius had started the auction gallery a year and a half ago and had quickly obtained success. Some of the items had come from their family's estate, which was presently being renovated, and the others were antiques that they acquired from various corners of the world.

Nicholas loved New York. His life in Romania had dwindled to routine boredom. This city had much to offer. He enjoyed the nightlife, the mixing of cultures and the many beautiful women who were willing to do anything to affiliate themselves with the wealthy. All of which he took complete advantage of.

The lid of the crate lifted and he eased it to the floor. He rummaged through the packing grass until he felt the smooth edges of the artifact that lay within. Carefully, he pulled it out and inspected it. The Rune of Moloch fit perfectly within the palm of his hand. For centuries it had been hidden within a secret chamber in his family's castle while its twin, the Rune of Cythe, had been secured by his father. By Lord Victor's orders the stones had always been kept apart, and if they were transported it was also done individually. As the castle was presently under renovations, Nicholas had decided to move the stone to a vault within the gallery to assure its security.

He turned to watch his brother standing next to his wife, who was busy admiring a collection of medieval jewelry. Marius was two years younger than him and about to be a father. Marius's young and beautiful wife, Alexandra, looked radiant despite being eight months pregnant.

Nicholas picked up his blazer, not bothering to slip it back on. He had to admit that he often found himself battling the green tentacles of envy when he compared his life to his brother's. Marius was married and in love. Nicholas habitually tried to convince himself that love and marriage weren't for him. He was a self-proclaimed rogue and enjoyed every moment of it. There were just too many delectable women out there in need of his attention.

Alexandra turned her bright eyes to Marius as he pulled a set of keys from his pocket. "Oh, no, I can't accept it," she protested as he leaned over to open the showcase.

Nicholas shook his head and turned away to

assess the work they'd done setting up the gallery. His brother was forever showering his wife with diamonds and emeralds, many of which were a part of their display and worth a hefty sum. If she saw something and took a fancy to it, then it was hers.

Nicholas snorted. He'd never doted on a woman so relentlessly. Then again, he and Marius were quite the opposite in most things. On the surface their relation was undeniable as they were tall, dark and striking—true to the Drakon bloodline. But Marius catered to their mother's disposition and was patient, gentle and thoughtful. Whereas Nicholas was intolerant, demanding and forceful. Yet, somehow they managed to work together and maintain a lucrative business.

Nicholas stalked out of the showroom toward the large vault at the rear of the gallery. He had no intention of keeping the rune stone in New York permanently, only holding it in the vault until the renovations in Romania were completed. When that time came he would return it to his brother Simion, who'd chosen to remain in their homeland.

He quickly punched in the security code at the vault's exterior door. He entered and did the same for the interior door. A small antique wooden box sat on one of the shelves to the right. He opened it carefully and set the rune inside. He left the room, securing the doors behind him.

When he returned to the showroom, Alexandra was lifting up her long black hair as Marius secured an elegant ninety-eight-carat sapphire necklace about her neck. Many years ago it had belonged to a countess. Now it would serve to accessorize the blue maternity dress Alexandra wore.

"Shall we be leaving soon?" he asked with a suppressed smirk.

"Yes," Marius replied. He turned Alexandra to face him and smiled with satisfaction. "You look lovely."

Her hazel eyes flashed with joy as she assessed her reflection in a small gilded mirror that sat on the top of the showcase. "It's beautiful!" She sent Nicholas a wary yet friendly look. "What do you think?"

Nicholas nodded his approval and experienced a pang of guilt when she quickly looked away. She had every reason to fear him. He only hoped that one day she'd be able to overlook the great wrong he'd done her and learn to trust him. His brother offered him a very wan but encouraging smile. Only time and patience would procure those results.

Nicholas flinched as an ache shot along his right hand. Of late, on nights like this when his emotions took precedence in his mind, he often experienced the same crippling ache in his joints and tasted the putrid bile that had always accompanied his transformation.

Whether he wanted to admit it or not, this unnerved him; a year and a half had passed since his family's curse should've been broken. However, there were many nights that he missed the liberties he'd enjoyed as a gargoyle. Nothing could compare to soaring through a star-strewn sky and surveying the quiet lands below. But he'd had his fill of becoming stone. The short thirty days he'd enjoyed as a man each year during the spring equinox—a pagan season that was marked by the sun's crossing over the celestial equator—hadn't prepared him for the freedom associated with humanity.

Marius shot him a curious look. "I see old age has finally taken a toll on you," he stated with a hint of amusement. "Perhaps you should consider a reprieve from all this." He turned and guided Alexandra toward the doorway.

Nicholas flexed his right hand, trying to subdue the cramping that was fast moving up his arm. "I am no more an old man than you," Nicholas returned with budding mirth.

His humor was short-lived as another ache shot up his arm and along his shoulders. He flexed his hand again. There was a chance that after so many years of enduring such a vicious cycle of being stone by day and gargoyle by night, his body was only lingering in its acclimation. Perhaps the dark creature he once was still lurked within him, looming in his subconscious, waiting to take possession. And if it was no longer being manipulated by the curse, then who or what was in command?

Daniela held her breath as she eased the two-inch-thick portion of glass out of place. She slid it to one side and detached the small suction device.

"Beautiful." She exhaled as she paused to admire her handiwork.

She prided herself on always having a clean entry, and the hole she'd burned through the skylight was just that. She stuffed the small laser into her backpack and pulled out another device. About the size of a matchbox and called the Defragmenter, it had the ability to disable any low-powered security defenses within a twenty-foot radius: cameras, lasers, motion-triggered bars.

She activated it, slipped it through the hole and attached it to the underside of the glass. Her equipment was always top of the line; a necessity for the complexity of her work.

Daniela lowered the rope she'd bolted to the roof. The Defragmenter beeped, signaling its completion. She detached it and used the rope to lower herself to the floor. Once on the ground, she activated the earpiece connected to her cell phone.

The voice of her best friend and partner in crime, Mai, greeted her. "You in yet?"

"I'm in."

She'd met Mai in New York's Chinatown two months after her mother's desertion. Mai had been a runaway, and it hadn't taken long for Daniela to become entangled in unscrupulous behavior. However, Mai had also been the one to introduce her to the local dojo. The sensei, taking pity on them, had offered the girls free

training, if only to aid them in protecting themselves. Daniela had become an avid student of
an art that she'd also excelled in.

Daniela shot a quick look about and confirmed what she already knew—the gallery was
deserted. She moved silently down the dimly
lit hall and toward the heavy door of the vault.
Mai had given her a complete blueprint of the
building and she knew that a security fence lay
behind the door. But she'd come prepared.

Pulling out her laptop computer and a small
battery-powered screwdriver from her backpack, she glanced at her watch. Once she started
tampering with the security control panel the
alarm would be triggered; she was sure the
Defragmenter wasn't capable of disabling something so complex.

Mai's voice invaded her ear again. "How are
you doing?"

"Ready to infiltrate," Daniela replied. "Looks
like we've got some state of the art equipment
here."

She quickly unscrewed the four screws that held the metal plate to the wall. She started the timer on her watch then quickly clipped the wires that connected the main computer to the panel. She stripped them and connected them to wires that were attached to her laptop. Immediately, a password request appeared on the monitor.

"Ok, I need a seven digit code. Do your thing."

"I'm on it."

A moment later numbers leapt to the screen, scrolling left to right in a random order. Daniela placed her laptop on the floor and waited.

Having a partner certainly made things easier. Mai always worked behind the scenes, as that was where her talents lay. She made all the connections, cracked all the computer codes, communicated with clients and infiltrated Chinatown's black market to purchase the latest in spy gear. The proceeds from every heist were always split fifty-fifty, and they used them for their own individual causes. Daniela chose to provide assistance to less fortunate families and children. She checked her watch just as the sound of locks being released could be heard. The heavy vault door eased open a crack. A smile crept to her lips. "Good job."

Nicholas slammed the door of his silver Lamborghini and stormed up the gallery steps. He'd received a call from the police only minutes before arriving home; the gallery had been broken into.

His scowl darkened as he pushed past the officers guarding the front entrance and marched through the marble archway that led into the gallery's vault. Marius stood at the exit, speaking with a detective.

Nicholas headed toward them. "What happened here?"

Marius looked up as he approached. "A thief entered through the roof only moments after we left. He disabled the cameras and was gone before the authorities arrived."

"What has been taken?" he asked.

Marius shot the detective a look then Nicholas, his eyes reflecting a contained measure of discontent. "The only item missing is the Rune of Moloch," he said.

Nicholas met his stare and uneasiness crept over him. He stepped around his brother to examine the tampered wires of the security panel. This had been no random act, he was sure. Why would any thief overlook all the priceless items within the gallery and steal only a stone with no apparent value? The heist had to have been contrived by one who knew the rune stone's significance.

The detective spoke then. "This isn't the first time something like this has happened." He extended a hand. "Detective Simmons."

Nicholas shook his hand and the detective continued.

"We have reason to believe that the thief who robbed you tonight is the Midnight Bandit. He's struck over twenty jewelry and antiques stores within the past year and his pattern is always the same—very clean entry, disables all secondary security devices within a twenty—or thirty-foot radius, hacks the main computer to gain access to the vaults, takes only one item and then disappears before the authorities arrive."

"And you have no knowledge of who is committing these crimes?" Nicholas asked.

"None. The thief never leaves fingerprints, DNA evidence or even eyewitnesses. One thing's for certain—this guy's really meticulous. We've only been following leads, most of which turn up empty."

"Have any of the stolen items ever been recovered?" Marius asked.

"Unfortunately, no. We have reason to believe they're channeled through the black market and out of the country."

Nicholas folded his arms across his broad chest. "So this 'Midnight Bandit' has been rampaging through the city for an entire year and yet you have no answers or solutions to offer?"

The detective's gaze flitted to Marius and back. "We just don't have the manpower to watch every potential target in this city. It's impossible. There's no budget for it. So we've been encouraging business owners like yourselves to take additional measures to protect your properties. It makes our job a little easier."

One of Nicholas's dark brows shot up. "And still you have yet to make progress?"

Marius cleared his throat. "I am certain you are doing everything you can. We will do whatever is necessary to assist you with your investigations." He sent Nicholas a pointed look.

Nicholas inclined his head and said no more. He allowed Marius to continue the interview while he headed toward the back of the gallery. He looked at the neat hole that had been left in the skylight above. The glass, he knew, was two inches thick. His gaze fell to the marble floor, combing it for any pieces that may have fallen, but found nothing.

He strayed over to the wide glass windows

and his gaze locked on to a point on the roof of the building across the street. They had no doubt been watched. His trepidation mounted. Somehow someone had learned that the rune would be delivered on that day and had devised a plan to steal it. Nicholas had been careful to keep news of its transport among only those who needed to know. This could mean only one thing: someone within their clan couldn't be trusted.

"Must you always be so embarrassing?" Marius's reflection appeared in the glass before him.

Nicholas shot him a glance over his shoulder. "One of the sacred runes has been stolen. I do not think my behavior warrants objection. There was a time when a thief stood no chance against the law. He was apprehended and sometimes beheaded right on the spot."

"In case you have not noticed, things have changed. Public decapitations would be sorely frowned upon. It is called being civilized. You would do well to embrace it."

He turned to face Marius. "The matter of this missing rune should not be taken lightly, brother. If it is so much as damaged the spell can be broken."

Marius looked pensive. "Father will not be pleased to hear of this. That secret has been buried within our family for many centuries. Whoever stole it must know of its importance."

Nicholas flexed his neck as a sudden ache began to move down his spine. "There are two possibilities. He intends only to attempt to harvest the power of the stone, for the knowledge of runes has not yet been forgotten. Or he is preparing to conjure the dark and ancient magic that retains the souls of our uncle and his followers. Either way it is a risk we cannot afford."

"And what of its twin?" Marius questioned. "The Rune of Cythe?"

"Only father knows its location."

Again Nicholas pondered the possibility of

one of their own bloodline plotting to break the spell. Surely the ruin that Gabriel had caused was no secret. To think that someone would wish to revive him was indeed disconcerting.

"I must travel to Romania," Nicholas told Marius.

"I will go with you," Marius offered.

"No, your wife needs you here."

Marius nodded. "And father?" His brows were furrowed with concern.

Nicholas sighed. "I will be the one to tell him." He sauntered back toward the hole in the skylight and peered up into it.

His eyes narrowed. The space was only large enough for a very slender form to pass through. He would've made mention of it, but a faint scent passed into his nostrils. He paused—it was barely present, a soft wisp of something pleasant.

Marius looked at him. "What is it?" he asked.

"There is a fragrance on the air."

Marius inhaled softly. "I smell nothing."

Nicholas realized that he was again tapping into the abilities he'd possessed as a gargoyle. He found it odd that Marius was unable to do the same.

"The air is laced with it," he told him as he inhaled deeply.

Marius followed. "What does it smell like?"

Nicholas was silent for a moment then he turned to face his brother. "Like roses."

Chapter 2

Drakon Castle, Romania

Nicholas flexed the thick and aching muscles of his neck. Obscured within the shadows of the large dining hall of his family's estate, he waited. He'd been pacing the darkness as he'd contemplated all the possible motives for what had occurred, when a noise had alerted him. Silently, he'd made his way down the hall, slipping an eighteenth-century rapier from the wall in the process.

He'd arrived in Romania earlier that day and had relayed the incident of the stolen rune stone to his father. As expected, Lord Victor hadn't taken the news well, and he'd summoned the elders of their clan to discuss the matter.

As Nicholas neared the main dining hall the scraping noise grew louder. He slipped within the shadows cast by the massive hearth whose jaws gaped with only slivers of a dying flame. From somewhere in the mansion a grandfather clock chorused the midnight hour. His eyes riveted to one of the tall rear windows and one thought invaded his mind—the Midnight Bandit had come to find the second rune.

A soft popping sound ensued and the window creaked open, the heavy drapes lifting as a gust of wind reached in to caress them. His muscles tensed. It had been a long time since he'd last had the privilege to engage in a worthwhile fight, and thus, he welcomed the inevitable confrontation with eagerness. He only hoped that his opponent was up to the challenge.

One black boot then another swung in through the opening. Nicholas would've advanced, but paused as two slender calves encased within skintight leather slipped in. Shapely thighs and hips followed. Dressed in a black, fitted shirt, leather pants and a mask, the figure landed in a silent crouch on the floor. His eyes narrowed on his new adversary. It seemed his assumption had been correct; the Midnight Bandit was female.

With feline grace, she crawled another few feet and she shot an assessing look about the room.

Nicholas remained as he was; still and without breath. He watched as she stood and began to saunter across the floor. She even took a moment to admire the room's heavy oak table before advancing. Her figure was completely outlined as she moved past the dull glow of the hearth.

Nicholas's gaze trailed the length of her as she drew nearer; lean and fit with full breasts and a slender waist. Her stride was bold and confident, that of one who had nothing to fear. It was obvious that she had no knowledge of the territory she'd chosen to invade.

He eased from the shadows then. "Five hundred years ago your crimes would have been punishable by death," he said.

Her attention snapped to him and a look of surprise crossed her eyes but she quickly regained her composure.

"I guess that makes me fortunate to be living in the present, doesn't it?"

One of Nicholas's dark brows peaked slightly at her sharp retort. "You would be wise to return the Rune of Moloch to me and save yourself the unnecessary grief."

Silence lapsed between them as she watched him. It was short-lived. "I have no intention of returning anything to you," she said. "In fact, I intend to walk out of here with the second one."

His eyes narrowed on her. A confrontation he'd anticipated, a fight he'd hoped for, but he hadn't expected this: a recalcitrant hoyden whose tongue was sharper than the blade he held.

"And I intend to stop you."

"It seems we have a conflict of interest." She quickly slid one of the brass fire pokers from its rack and took a defensive martial arts stance.

"So it seems." With fluid grace he raised his own weapon just in time to block her attack. Metal met metal in a deafening clash that initiated a fierce waltz. Her speed and agility both surprised and impressed him. She moved with the apparent effortlessness of one well schooled in the art. He found himself wondering who she was. The world had softened and its warriors had abandoned the ancient arts of physical combat. She was a rarity indeed.

She attacked again, slicing upward. Nicholas jumped backward, but not before the sharp point of the fire poker slipped up along the front of his billowed shirt. The material fell apart, gaping to reveal his midsection.

"If you intend to stop me you'd better try

harder than that," she said with a smirk in her voice.

Nicholas gripped his shirt and tore it from his body. If she wanted a fight she was going to get one. He charged forward, but she evaded his attack with a graceful backward flip. It seemed the bandit was also an accomplished gymnast.

She returned the favor with an attack of her own, swinging her weapon in a manner that would've disabled a man of lesser skill. But he was prepared for her this time. He evaded her assault and gripped the top of her ninja-style mask, stripping it from her head.

A wealth of inky tendrils fell about her face and shoulders like a cloud of hellfire smoke. Eyes of the same haunting hue locked with his as she eased back a step.

Nicholas stared, his gaze unabashed and lustful, for the creature before him was more than beautiful. She was exotic and striking, an apparition of complete and utter perfection. Desire ignited within him. He'd never met a woman whose skill rivaled her beauty.

"Who are you?" he asked quietly.

For a moment he thought he would gain no response, and then she spoke. "Does it matter?"

He was given no time to respond for she came at him again, brandishing her weapon in a way that would've made her teacher proud. Nicholas matched her speed, but was careful to only block her attack. Although he relished the throes of battle, he didn't believe in harming those weaker than himself. And this little delinquent, although well trained, was no match for his five centuries of ruthless grooming.

He ducked an attack then swept a foot beneath her. His sudden move was unexpected and she lost her balance, coming to land flat on her back. Nicholas marched toward her and quickly kicked the fire poker aside. She moved to sit up, but he crouched above her and placed a firm hand against her chest.

He watched her in the dim lighting. She lay

still, her breathing coming in quick gasps. His gaze trailed her body, moving along the ripe curves of her breasts, down her flat abdomen to the tight and very suggestive molding of her pants. He found himself wondering what sort of undergarments, if any at all, could be worn beneath the skintight attire. A low groan escaped him and he was abruptly reminded of how long it had been since he'd last had a woman; nearly two days now. He was ravenous.

Daniela fought to catch her breath as she gazed up at the tall figure towering above her. Two days after the heist of the Rune of Moloch, she'd received word from Mai that the same buyer wanted an artifact that was identical to the first. He had only the assumption that the rune was hidden within Drakon Castle, which meant she was left with the daunting task of trying to locate it. But he was paying double; a fair enough arrangement in her books. She'd immediately left for Romania, leaving her sister Elaina, who was now fifteen, under Mai's supervision.

She'd been waiting outside the castle for hours. She'd deduced that only one person was at the residence, and when all the lights had dimmed, she'd made her move. She hadn't expected to find one of the Drakon brothers waiting for her in the darkness—and with a sword.

She'd played it off well and kept her cool, but even now her heart, along with her mind, raced. She'd never been caught before, and at this point the possibility of an escape seemed nonexistent. Time and time again she'd promised herself to give up stealing, but it was the only way of life she knew. Now it was too late. It seemed her rope had just come to an abrupt end.

The man responsible stood above her for what seemed an eternity, his transfixing green eyes piercing into her. Finally, he spoke.

"Where is the Rune of Moloch?" It was an unmistakable command.

Daniela, however, was determined not to convey exactly what she was feeling. "Sold by now, I would imagine." She was also making a valiant effort to keep her eyes from flitting along the broad expanse of his well-muscled torso.

"Sold to whom?" he asked, his gaze unrelenting.

Daniela stared back. Did he honestly think she would just tell him what he wanted to know? She was already going to be imprisoned for her crimes. The last thing she needed was to have her name out on the street as the one who spilled her guts. She didn't know the identity of the buyer, but the men who'd collected the item weren't exactly prize citizens. They were the scourge of the criminal world, and she didn't want to find out just how dirty they could get. If he wanted answers he was going to have to find them himself.

It seemed he read her stubborn resolve, for in a swift movement he sheathed his sword and reached down, pulling her to her feet.

"You will tell me what I wish to know and

you will do so now," he said as he spun her to face the wall.

With her hands pressed against the cool stone, Daniela steeled herself to remain still as he begun stripping her of her weapons and gadgets. "Why should I waste my time? The way I see it, I've got nothing left to lose."

She could feel the intense heat of his powerful form as he reached around her to slip her phone from her waistband.

"Nay, girl," his deep voice vibrated throughout her body and his warm breath invaded her ear. "There is much you have yet to lose."

A large hand moved slowly up along the ripe curve of her hip as he felt the pockets there. Daniela clenched her teeth. She knew that it was more than obvious that she carried nothing there. The material was, after all, like a second skin.

His hand glided higher, up her slender waist and to her chest. She struck the offending member away. "I have nothing hidden there," she gritted out.

Something resembling a snicker reverberated within his chest. "One can never tell with you women." He braced an arm above her head and leaned over her. "You may begin your recount," he told her.

Daniela cast him a brief look over her shoulder. She didn't know what was worse, his pompous attitude or the scorching heat that was passing through the entire length of her back. She was determined to appear impassive. Her effort might've worked too, had he not turned on her cell phone.

The device chimed softly as the light flickered on. His attention was drawn to the image on the screen and she found that she was suddenly embarrassed. She'd uploaded the image a few days ago; it was of her and her sister at the orphanage's Easter party.

He hovered above her, quiet and contemplative. Daniela lowered her forehead against the cool wall. She certainly wasn't proud of the life she'd chosen to continue, especially when so many looked up to her. She didn't know how she would ever face them all if she went to jail for burglary.

He snapped her phone off and slipped it into his pocket. "You can take your chances with me or with the authorities," he told her, his tone incomprehensible.

Daniela knew within herself that there was nothing to consider. If she continued to resist he would call the police and have her arrested. But if she went along with him she could gain enough time to execute an escape.

"Fine," she agreed. "What do you want to know?"

His free hand moved to the exposed skin between her fitted shirt and low-rise pants. Calloused fingers traced slowly along her skin. "Who are you employed under?"

Fighting the tingling sensation that was fast spreading from the spot where his fingers played, Daniela rationed the air within her lungs. "I work for no one."

His fingers paused on her hip. "Then what compels you to steal?"

"Money, what else? I have responsibilities."

His fingers began to move again, this time outlining the edge of her leather pants. "That is hardly an excuse."

Her eyes narrowed and she bit down hard on her retort. What did he know of responsibilities? Born into such a wealthy family he'd no doubt had everything given to him. She despised his kind.

"Who have you sold the Rune to? And did he hire you to steal the second?" His finger encountered her slinky thong and he looped a finger into one of the straps, pulling it further to the surface.

She inhaled slowly. She wondered how he'd managed to assume that she'd taken the missing rune stone. She'd been careful to cover her tracks. Her heart began to race again. She wasn't sure if it was due to the uncanny fact that this man knew far too much about her activities or to the warm sensations he was stirring within her.

When she provided no response, he looped his finger within the strap of her thong a second time, tightening the undergarment. "Answer me, girl."

"I don't know him," she managed. "But yes, he wants the second rune."

His deep groan echoed within his chest as he acknowledged her admission. "Now I will ask you again, who is this buyer? You steal upon his request. You must know something of him."

"I've never seen him," she breathed. "I only steal the items and they tell me where to make the drop-offs," she blurted.

"Where?"

"About thirty minutes from here is an old monastery. I'm expected to deliver the second rune there tomorrow night."

"You will take me there now."

She tossed him a look over her shoulder, her brows drawn in a frown. "I don't have the rune and there's no way I'm going there without it."

"You will lead me to this location, but not under the pretense of delivering the rune," he told her. "I wish to see this drop-off point that you speak of."

"I don't think so," she shook her head. "You don't get it, do you? This isn't some game of cops and robbers. These men will kill me if they even suspect that I've betrayed them."

He leaned in closer, the heat of his body searing a hole through the clothes at her back. "There you are wrong. This is a game—one that you initiated and one you will see to its end." He spoke evenly, but it was clear that he would abide no objections.

Daniela remained silent for a moment, definitely not liking the way things were progressing. Going to any drop-off unannounced and empty-handed was risky. She wouldn't only be placing herself in danger, but also those closest to her. She knew all too well the kind of people she did business with. They were a dangerous group and were loyal only to the highest bidder. And when they were crossed they stopped at nothing, cutting down everything and anything in their paths until they got what they wanted. She would never forgive herself if anything ever happened to the people she loved.

Yet there was no way she was going to jail either. All in all, she had no easy way out of this. She would continue to go along with whatever he asked until she could make a run for it.

Daniela's head fell against the cool stone wall and she sighed in resignation. "Fine, I'll take you there."

A deep groan rumbled within his chest as he acknowledged her acquiescence. It passed through her rib cage and slid up her spine. At that moment he slipped his finger from the binds of her thong and the strap retracted with a snap.

The heat of his body left her as he stepped

back. Slowly, she turned to face him. He stepped to one side and motioned for her to lead the way out of the room, his eyes daring her to try something. Reluctantly, Daniela moved forward. Her heart was drumming. She steeled herself to remain calm, but something told her that this was going to be a very long night.

Chapter 3

Daniela pulled the motorcycle helmet off and exhaled a slow breath as she freed her hair. The ride to the drop-off point had been more than uncomfortable since she'd been forced to sit astride the sleek black motorcycle behind her captor. She'd been careful to avoid as much physical contact as possible, but with less than an inch between them that had proven to be an impossible task.

She slid from the rear of the motorcycle and turned her attention to the lights that could be seen flickering several yards beyond the trees. They were from the Branchovan Monastery.

She'd scouted it earlier in the day, yet the ghastly structure still sent shivers coursing down her spine. Nestled at the base of a sloping hill, it was surrounded by a forest on one side and the lifeless expanse of a shadowy lake on the other. Centuries ago it had been a place of holy devotion, and now it served as a storage facility and exchange point for stolen goods.

Within the shrouding darkness of the trees, her captor's silhouette appeared at her side. Nicholas, he'd said his name was. She'd given him her name, not that it mattered anyway. He'd returned the majority of her possessions to her, but kept her cell phone and she was certain his intent was to learn her true identity.

Ignoring the odd fluttering at the pit of her stomach as he drew nearer, she put on her night-vision binoculars. Several of the monastery's windows were illuminated and she could see several men inside, stacking and moving crates around.

"I don't know how you think you're going to

get in there. The place is crawling with security," she told him.

Nicholas eased a branch aside and fixed his attention to the structure below. "By the design I feel safe to assume that it is more than several hundred years old. It was considered essential to have an alternate and hidden point of access as no one was exempt from the savage sieges that had plagued the land. Not even those of the cloth." He let the branch fall back into place. "Come, we will find another entrance."

Daniela fixed him with a questioning look. "We? I never agreed to go down there with you."

His gaze fell over her. "You agreed to take me to the place you were instructed to deliver the rune."

"And I did. Why do you think we're here? For sightseeing?"

The delay in his response lingered a moment longer than it should have; with the darkness to obscure the emotion on his face, she wondered if she was crossing the line of his good graces.

"Should I so readily accept the words of a thief? One whom I found stealing her way into my family's home?" He moved closer, swallowing any space between them. "We are going into the monastery. Please do not mistake this for a request."

Daniela's eyes narrowed on him as she fought the retort that was fast climbing within her throat. He towered above her, his face partially illuminated by a slanted bar of light that had stolen access through the trees. Emerald eyes flashed. He looked dangerous. Not one to be crossed.

Without waiting for her response, he moved toward his motorcycle and removed the keys then the huge crossbow that was strapped to one side. He stalked past her to begin the descent down the steep hill. Daniela glared after him, her temper mounting. Had she known he expected her to accompany him on whatever in-

sane mission he had planned, she would've attempted an escape long before now. But it was
too late. They were miles away from anything
and with no vehicle at her disposal any such
move would be foolish. She was here and would
have to comply with his wishes. Reluctantly,
she sighed and kept to the cover of the trees as
she followed him.

It wasn't long before they reached the back of
the monastery. Surrounded by tall and ancient
trees that yawned into the night and shrouded
the towering walls, it was no less welcoming.
The scent of earth, moist and decaying, hung
about them. Daniela inhaled a shaky breath and
blamed the racing of her heart on the steady
pace of her descent.

Nicholas stood a few feet from her, his eyes
combing the base of the wall as if they could
penetrate the heavy shadows. He bent and
brushed the leaves from a spot on the ground
before scooping up a handful of soil.

"The land here is low," he spoke quietly. "If

there is a passage beneath the monastery it would no doubt be saturated by the lake." He discarded the soil and moved to another spot.

Daniela watched with curiosity as he repeated this again. Despite herself, she couldn't help but admire the easy grace with which he moved. Their confrontation was still burned within her mind and she found herself wondering where he'd acquired his skills. Of course he was of noble birth—that would explain his swordsmanship. There was no training money couldn't buy, but there was something more about him that made her curious; something that hinted to a deviant or less than normal lifestyle. Whatever it was, she was certain it wasn't done out of need. It was obvious that Nicholas Drakon hadn't needed anything in his entire life, except maybe a good time-out.

"Here," he said and beckoned her to him. "The soil is overly damp. There must be a passage that runs to the other side."

Daniela knelt and tested the soil for herself.

He was right. The soil was nearly mud. Even the leaves that were strewn above it left moisture on her fingertips.

He stood and headed toward the towering wall of the monastery. Daniela followed and watched as he began pulling aside the entanglement of vines and bushes that grew along the wall. She reached into her boot and pulled out a flashlight. As she approached him she heard the sound of decayed wood ripping away.

She switched on the light to aid him. With one heavy boot braced against the wall, he was ripping a hole through the planks of rotten wood that had been nailed to the structure. Beyond them she could see the entrance of a dark passage. Stale air poured out and the trickling sound of water could be heard.

Nicholas turned to face her. "This passage should take us inside."

"I need a weapon," she told him. When he only stared at her she continued. "If something happens in there I want to at least be able to defend myself."

Nicholas watched her for a moment longer then slipped an item from his back pocket. He tossed it to her. Daniela caught it without effort then pinned him with an incredulous look.

"What the hell am I supposed to do with this?" she asked.

The pocket knife he'd given her was lovely with a silver handle that had been carved with various Celtic symbols. However, it was no more than four inches long.

What appeared to be humor crossed his face. "It is a weapon, is it not?"

Her attention moved to the large crossbow he'd just stripped from his back. "Looks more like a Christmas ornament," she commented with sarcasm. "I can't defend myself with this."

He laughed then; a low, deep and very sensuous sound. He sauntered toward her and slipped the flashlight from her fingers. "Then you are just going to have to trust me to do it for you."

Daniela could only stare at him. He certainly was a beautiful man. It was a pity he didn't have a personality to match. She must've lingered too long without a response for he jerked his head toward the entrance.

With every effort to maintain a calm disposition, she moved and ducked into the passageway.

The small flashlight cast its light about the tunnel, revealing a gravel floor and concave brick walls that were laden with moss. A path of water lined the center of the ground beneath them, no doubt the seepage from the river.

In silence they walked for a few minutes. Daniela listened intently for any noise that would indicate they'd somehow been discovered. Her heart drummed within her chest as they advanced deeper into the shadows. If she got out of this one unscathed she was quitting her thieving ways for sure.

Nicholas paused and Daniela realized that the passage had narrowed to a crawl space that was a few feet off the ground. He angled the light and peered in. "This is the only way in," he told her.

Daniela eyed the passage. They would have to crawl through, and the last thing she wanted was to be bent over in front of him. "And I suppose you expect me to go in first?"

A flash of humor registered in his eyes. "I do not trust you at my back so I would have it no other way." He offered her a hand.

With an exasperated sigh she ignored him and gripped the edge of the passage, pulling herself up and inside. Kneeling, she turned and slipped her flashlight from his hand, glaring at him. The light revealed that the passage went on for at least another twenty feet. What lay beyond that she couldn't tell.

A soft noise behind her told Daniela that Nicholas had joined her in the passage. His huge frame seemed to fill the entire space and she suddenly felt like a caged animal. She'd never been prone to claustrophobia, but it was becoming increasingly difficult to breathe. Shaking her head to clear her thoughts, she focused on the path ahead and began to crawl forward.

They'd only gone a moderate distance when she felt a cooling draft teasing the stray locks of her hair that had managed to escape the confines of her ponytail. She brought the light up to see a rusty metal fence in front of her. Peering through the bars, she did a quick sweep of the room beyond. It was large and filled with unmarked wooden crates.

"Can you get through the gate?" Nicholas asked from behind her.

She turned the light to the fence, finding that its roots lay imbedded into the wall. "I'll see." She set the flashlight down and gripped the bars, applying her full weight against it, but it was in vain. The bars simply wouldn't budge.

Repositioning slightly, she braced one boot against it and tried again. Flakes of brittle rust cracked away, but as before the bars held firm.

"Allow me to try," Nicholas offered.

Daniela looked at him then at the space they were allotted. There was no way he was going to get around her. He must've realized their dilemma simultaneously for he backed up suddenly.

"Lie on your back," he told her. "I will climb over you."

She blinked at him. *Could the night get any worse?* As if being squeezed into the narrow passage with him wasn't bad enough, now she would have to endure his very large and hard body sliding over her own. Reluctantly, she complied.

Nicholas moved over her and the heat of his body immediately assailed her as he came to a kneeling position just over her. He leaned forward, increasing her torment as his long hair spilled over his shoulders to tease the sensitive skin of her face. Never had she been this close to a man or in such a compromising position. She hated to admit it, but this pompous man had ignited a fire within her and she wanted nothing more than to stamp it out.

"Cover your eyes," he told her as he gripped the bars.

With her eyes closed tightly, Daniela could feel the exact moment when the thick corded muscles of his thighs clenched, and seconds later a crumbling noise ensued. Opening her eyes slowly, she cast a look over her head to find that the metal fence had been completely ripped from the wall.

Nicholas had to lean forward a bit more so that he could allow the iron to carefully slide to the floor below. This action brought his face mere inches from her own. His very masculine scent engulfed her, slipping into her nostrils to toy with her imagination.

The metal fence scrapped its way down the wall and landed on the floor with a quiet clank. Nicholas's eyes met and held her own and he watched her for a few seconds. In this lighting they looked black, but she remembered from their earlier encounter that they were a very transfixing green; the color of the Brazilian rain forest after a fresh rain. His gaze was contemplative as he watched her, assessing almost.

"From this point on you will obey me without question," he told her quietly. "Is that understood?"

Daniela was silent for a moment. She'd never been inclined to take orders from anyone, and she certainly wasn't appreciating his demanding nature. But in her present predicament she would have to contend with it. She nodded.

He acknowledged her compliance with a grunt then moved carefully over her and through the exit. Daniela remained motionless for a moment as she regained her composure, then she quickly followed. Nicholas was moving between the crates, scrolling the light over them.

Daniela moved to stand beside him. "I don't think you're going to find the rune anywhere in this monastery," she told him. "These guys are just middlemen. They acquire the items for the buyers and I'm not sure what happens after that, but I don't think they keep them lying about for too long."

"You may be correct, but as you say they are middlemen and at present my only connection to the one who has the rune."

He turned and headed toward a short flight of stone steps that lead to a doorway outlined by a dull orange glow. He gripped the door handle and it turned with ease.

Daniela moved up the steps to join him then waited as he pulled the door open a crack and peered through. He listened for a few seconds and when they were met with quiet, he pulled the door wider. Dull light poured in from the narrow passage that lay beyond. They entered quietly and moved toward another flight of steps. A wooden door stood at the top of the stairway. As before, Nicholas eased it open and they looked through.

They heard muffled voices but no one was within sight. They slipped past the threshold and into a long, wide hall lit by several dangling bulbs. They moved cautiously toward an archway that was aglow with a light from a lower floor.

Daniela matched Nicholas's pace, staying close, but never advancing ahead. Oddly, she didn't feel any fear. There was just something about the man that gave her a sense of reassurance. She wasn't sure if it was the confidence in his stride, the way he held his crossbow at his side—subtly poised for anything—or his tall and powerful frame. Whatever the reason, it was certainly an odd feeling for her. Never had she met a man who made her feel anything remotely close to security.

They passed through the archway and found themselves on the second floor of the main hall. The upper level was lined with a banister while the foyer below was crowded with wooden crates and barrels. Five men moved about, stacking the crates and rolling the barrels to one side.

Nicholas assumed an immediate crouching position and Daniela followed suit. Concealed within the shadows and behind the wooden posts of the banister, they observed the scene below. The men spoke with British accents and Daniela recognized one of them immediately. Tall and with a gangly frame, she knew him only by his nickname, Cradle. She'd done business with him a few times, actually delivering the first rune to him a few days ago. And it was to him that she was expected to deliver the second.

"That's him," she told Nicholas. "He's the one I gave the rune to."

He fixed the man with a lethal look. "So it is possible that the rune is here?"

Daniela didn't like the look on his face. It seemed he contemplated a confrontation. Between him with his antique weapon and her with her butter knife, the chances of victory were positively slim.

"No," she tried to dissuade. "I told you before

that these guys are just middlemen. I doubt they hold on to the items for very long."

"He was given the rune. If it is not in his possession he will know where it is." With that he slid forward a few feet.

Daniela watched him incredulously. There was no way he could confront Cradle without alerting the others. And doing that would only lead to his death—or worse.

She cast a glance over her shoulder. It was time for her to make an exit. Nicholas had her cell phone and could possibly use it to learn her identity, but if she managed to get out of there she could contact Mai and have her cancel her cellular account. Attempting an escape was better than remaining here to face a certain death. Even if Nicholas didn't make it out of there, her life was still at risk because her cell phone remained in his pocket, which she was sure Cradle and his comrades would search.

She briefly considered returning the way they'd come, but realized that it would take too long to reach a safe distance. What she needed was a fast and easy escape route. Her gaze flitted across the upper level of the room, scanning the shadows as she sought an alternative exit. It seemed luck was on her side for on the opposite end of the room a small glass window beckoned to her. It was slightly ajar and just wide enough for her to pass through. The only problem was that she'd never be able to make her way to it before she got caught. But then she'd always been innovative.

Again she scanned the room. Overhead the ancient ceiling had been left open and she could see the heavy maze of rafters. She was certain she could reach them, and the beams looked sturdy enough to support her weight.

She shot a glance at the men below, then to Nicholas. She would have only a few seconds before he realized that she'd left his side. Her plan would have to be executed without flaw. In the next second, she stood, climbed onto the banister and made a jump for the nearest beam of the rafter. She caught it and gracefully swung her legs up and around it, finally pulling her entire body onto it.

Slipping into a feline crouch, her gaze swept over the occupants of the room a second time. The men below went about their duties, but Nicholas's very disapproving attention was pinned to her. A smirk tugged at the corner of her mouth and she shrugged. There was no way he could follow her and he knew it.

She turned and began her careful journey toward the window. She'd only gotten midway when the beam beneath her began to creak. She froze. The sound had been very quiet, barely audible beneath the laughter of the men below, but she'd heard it. And oddly, so had Nicholas. She looked at him just in time to see his eyes dip to the beam. A quick assessment revealed that, although the beam itself was sturdy, the joints that connected it were worn with decay.

The wood creaked again and she weighed her options; going back was definitely not among them. Besides, she was halfway to the other side. She only needed to be quick, she told herself, to make it there.

One, she began counting, *two, three...*

She made a dash for it, got only another few feet before a loud creak resounded across the room and the termite-riddled joints that held the beam up surrendered to the added weight. Daniela gripped a smaller beam over her head, but that too gave way and she found herself falling to the ground.

She landed gracefully amidst the lengths of rotten wood. Dust hung about her and as she stood she looked up to find the five men, including Cradle, watching her. She slowly backed toward a stack of crates as they advanced. Her heart began drumming wildly when one of them pulled out a gun.

"Well, well. What have we got here?" he said.

"Looks like a little spy," said another.

"Or the police," Cradle piped in.

Daniela made an effort to keep her eyes

averted from him. He'd never seen her face as she'd always worn her mask during drop-offs, but she didn't want to take any chances. If by some twist of fate she did make it out of there alive, she didn't want Cradle tracking down her friends and family.

She eased back another few steps, but was halted when the gunman raised his weapon.

"Stop right there," he barked. "Who sent you here?" When she didn't respond he cocked the gun. "I asked you a question."

Before Daniela could provide a response, an arrow zipped through the air and penetrated the gunman's right shoulder. He cried out in agony and the gun toppled to the floor. All eyes turned toward the top of the stairway just in time to see Nicholas leap over the banister. He landed effortlessly on his feet then brought the hind end of his crossbow square in the face of the man nearest him. With a cry the man stumbled backward and into a stack of crates.

It took the others only a few seconds to assess

this new threat and one of the men snatched up the gun, aiming for Nicholas's chest. Daniela intercepted his attack with a kick to the midsection that knocked the wind out of him. The gun went off and a sharp pain shot through her left thigh.

The fight that transpired after that could only be described as chaos. The three men who remained on their feet charged at them, wielding anything they could get their hands on. Daniela quickly put her martial arts training into use while Nicholas fired off two more arrows, disabling another opponent. He discarded his weapon then and went at it fist to fist with his next attacker.

Despite their present predicament, Daniela couldn't help but admire the speed and agility with which Nicholas fought. He moved as a man who'd been well trained in the art of combat. His opponent was easily defeated and Nicholas snatched up his crossbow again, turning to watch as she finished her attacker with a blinding blow to the head.

Their eyes met as she remained kneeled over the motionless figure, forcing her breathing to assume a steady rhythm. He stared at her for a few seconds longer, his gaze hard and indiscernible. It was all Daniela could do not to flinch. She didn't fear him and wasn't going to give him the satisfaction of thinking she did.

He didn't bark orders at her as she'd expected. Instead, he turned and marched toward Cradle who was holding his wounded arm.

With his boot, Nicholas rolled Cradle over onto his back. "The Rune of Moloch, where is it?"

Cradle spat, sending a tooth bouncing to the floor. "I don't know what you're talking about," he said as he tried to sit up.

Nicholas reached down and slipped an arrow from the quiver strapped to his leg. "It was given to you. Now where is it? This is your final opportunity to respond." He positioned the arrow into the bow.

Daniela looked at her left thigh. She'd been shot. A small hole had been ripped into her leather pants and blood seeped through. She looked around quickly and spotted a large canvas drape that was piled on the floor. She crawled toward it and used Nicholas's knife to cut a length of it which she then fastened tightly around her thigh, grimacing as the pain intensified.

She pushed herself to her feet and briefly considered another escape, but decided against it. Nicholas was clearly very skilled with the weapon he held. And with her injured leg she wasn't likely to get very far. As for how a man of the twenty-first century had acquired such precision with an antique weapon, she couldn't imagine. Nevertheless, his disposition was hardly one to be tested.

Cradle had managed to drag himself a few inches toward a stack of crates. His brow was furrowed in suspicion and his eyes darted to her and back. Daniela quickly averted her gaze, silently cursing Nicholas's tactless interrogation. Few people knew that Cradle had collected the rune and she only hoped that the number was large enough to exempt her from suspicion.

Nicholas aimed his weapon and his finger eased on the trigger. A flash of lightning from outside illuminated the room and the lazy rumble of thunder quickly ensued. A storm approached.

Cradle eyed the man above him warily and a lump forced its way down his throat. "Hey, I only collected the item. I don't know where it is now."

"Who did you give it to?"

"I took it to a campsite about ten miles on the outskirts of Bucharest. I'd never been there before and never seen the two women I gave it to," he admitted.

"Two women?" Nicholas questioned.

"Yeah," Cradle continued as he repositioned

himself, supporting his obviously deformed wrist with his uninjured hand. "Two broads. Twins by the look of them—real stiff-lipped Addams Family rejects."

"And what were you given in exchange for the rune?"

"Money. That's all these jobs are to me—a paycheck. I don't ask questions. I just do what I'm told."

Nicholas remained poised over the man for a few seconds then grunted in response as he stepped back. "Get up," he ordered.

Cradle crawled to his feet. Without a word Nicholas jerked his head toward a large crate that sat open on the floor. Cradle understood and although a look of reluctance crossed his face, he complied without question. With much difficulty he climbed into the crate and fell back into the packing grass.

Nicholas set his crossbow aside and swung the heavy wooden lid up. "Your associates should be awake by sunrise. I am sure they will discover you here," he told Cradle before setting the lid into place.

He marched toward another crate and picked it up, putting it firmly onto the lid of the first, securing Cradle inside. Daniela exhaled softly. At least no one had been killed. She wasn't quite sure of what to expect from Nicholas Drakon. Her relief was shortlived when he snatched up his crossbow and turned his attention to her.

Propping the weapon up onto his shoulder, he sauntered toward her, pausing a few feet away. He stood there watching her, his eyes narrowed as they trailed the length of her. Daniela tried to still the racing of her heart, but couldn't. The man simply looked dangerous with his long mane of dark hair spilling over his back and shoulders. With as much bravado as she could muster, she waited for his next move.

His eyes dipped over her again "You have been wounded," he said in a low voice.

"It's nothing," she lied even as another sharp pain shot down her leg.

"There are medications at the estate. We can treat it there," he told her as he pulled the bow from his shoulder and began to disable it.

Daniela blinked. What the hell was he talking about? He'd gotten what he wanted and it didn't seem as if he intended to turn her in to the police. There was absolutely no reason for her to remain with him.

"I've shown you what you wanted to see. I'd like to go now," she said with more confidence than she felt. "Oh, and I need my phone back."

Nicholas's hand paused on the crossbow and he looked up at her. Emerald eyes flashed. "Dawn is nearly upon us," he said. "I intend to be back at the estate before the sun rises. I do not have the patience or the time to spare." He motioned toward the main entry door with his crossbow.

As she'd done so many times that night, Daniela swallowed her comment. She hated to admit it, but there was something about Nicholas Drakon that made her insides quiver.

It was like a sordid mixture of anger and intense attraction. She'd never been immediately drawn to anyone before, most especially someone of the opposite sex. It was a pity he was such a nuisance to be around. And it seemed she would have to endure even more of his less-than-winning disposition.

Trying to ignore the pain in her leg, she headed toward the main exit. Nicholas extended a hand to assist her, but she shoved it away. She didn't need his help.

Chapter 4

Nicholas shoved through the door of the estate's kitchen. He was in a foul mood. Not only had Daniela nearly gotten them both killed, but for the price of learning very little about the location of the missing rune. And to top it all off, they'd not managed to escape a sudden storm and were presently soaking wet.

Daniela's knees buckled just as they entered the room and he caught her before she touched the floor. She was no doubt weakened by the fair amount of blood she'd lost.

"Sit," he instructed as he guided her into the room.

Daniela complied, seating herself at the polished mahogany table that sat in the center of the kitchen. Matching countertops and cupboards lined one side of the room and a small couch sat near the rear wall.

Nicholas headed for a cupboard and returned with a wooden box and a bottle of brandy. He looked at the blood-soaked rag that she'd used as a makeshift tourniquet. The bleeding had stopped. Carefully, she released the knot that secured it into place and bit down on her bottom lip, but remained silent. Nicholas could tell that although she hid it well she was in much pain.

He placed the box on the table and opened the lid. It contained medicinal items from a modern first aid kit and a few that were similar to those used in the 1900s. He went to the sink and returned with a bowl of water.

"I will need to clean your wound and the bullet must be extracted. Remove your pants," he told her.

Her attention snapped to him. "I don't think so," she told him flatly.

His eyes narrowed on her. The wound was bound to become infected if it wasn't tended to, and he needed her alive and well. He was sure that she would be contacted the following night once she didn't show up with the second rune. His plan was simple. He would have her admit to encountering trouble, but state that she'd managed to steal the rune anyway. As the monastery would no longer be deemed a safe haven and the delivery of the item would already be late, he would have her offer to deliver the stone to the source itself. "Remove your pants or I will remove them for you," he warned.

Their eyes locked, hers relaying a fierce defiance. He could see her weighing her options. It was futile to defy him for it was he who determined her fate. Her jaw hardened and he knew that she'd come to this very conclusion.

With a dark scowl that made her sleek brows

pucker, she used the table for support and pushed to her feet. She stared up at him, her head barely level with his chin. When he remained as he was she let out an exasperated sigh that made her ample chest rise temptingly.

"Can you at least give me some privacy?" she asked.

Nicholas pondered the humor of her request. She could certainly be amusing in all her tartness. To think that he would turn his back on her a second time was foolish.

"I assure you, you have nothing I have not seen before." He brought his arms up to cross over his chest. "Proceed."

If possible, her eyes grew even more venomous. "You arrogant *son of a bitch,*" she gritted out as she jerked the single button at her waistband open.

"Spoken like a true criminal deviant," he countered.

He watched as she yanked the zipper down, revealing a surprisingly lacy thong. What he'd originally thought was white turned out to be a soft pink. There was even a little bow fastened to the band. His gaze trailed to her face as she pushed the left leg carefully over her injury. It seemed there lay some softness beneath her calloused exterior after all.

With her pants rolled to her knees she eased back into the chair. Nicholas assumed it was her pride that prevented her from trying to conceal the beautiful curve of her hips and thighs. She sat still even as he kneeled before her and removed a packet of gauze from the kit then began swabbing at the blood that had dried about the point of entry.

"You would do well to take a drink of that brandy," he suggested.

Daniela shook her head. "No, thanks. I'll need all my wits about me in case you try something."

His gaze slid to her face. "If it was my intent *to try something,* no measure of wit would save you, be assured."

She was silent, no doubt absorbing his words. "Funny," she said at last. "For someone with so much money you certainly weren't taught very many manners."

He snorted. "Scolded by a woman who makes her living stealing from others. How I have fallen," he scoffed.

His humor wasn't taken well and her eyes narrowed on him. "Why are you holding me here? To torture me with your sarcasm?" she asked.

He studied her for a moment, noting the way her damp hair had curled about her face and shoulders. "You have not served your full purpose yet," he told her. "You are my only hope of finding the rune and the one who hired you to steal it. Until I do, you will remain here."

"I believe that's called kidnapping."

He nodded in agreement. "Perhaps it is, but you are hardly in the position to alert the authorities, are you?" Without waiting for her response, he dipped a fresh wad of gauze into the bowl and moved lower on her thigh. He noted another small bullet hole. It could've been an exit wound, but it was curiously small. He would have to be certain. He removed a small pair of forceps from the kit.

"This will hurt, but I will be done with it as quickly as I can."

"Just get it over with," she snapped.

Nicholas watched her curiously. He'd been thoroughly impressed by her fighting skill and her courage. She had a hard strength about her that wasn't ordinarily seen in women of the modern era. This, coupled with her beautiful face and form made her quite desirable. But this was business. His family's future was at stake and he would have no dealings with the one who was partially responsible for bringing it down upon them. Not that she would permit it anyway. The woman was a shrew.

Taking the forceps he began to gently fish around the anterior wound. Her grip tightened on the edge of the chair and she looked away, but refrained from crying out. Having done this sort of thing many times before over the centuries, Nicholas quickly discerned that the bullet had indeed exited her body.

"You were quite fortunate," he told her.

He wiped the area a second time then removed a small pouch from the box. He opened it and the aroma of dried leaves poured out.

"What's that?" Daniela asked suspiciously.

"It's called kava," he informed. "The plant is dried and has been used as a topical anesthetic for centuries."

Pinching a small portion out of the bag, he applied it to her wound then proceeded to place a bandage about her thigh. His fingers grazed her skin a few times and he was hard-pressed to ignore how extremely soft she felt. Her body was perfect; ripe and smooth. He found himself wishing that they'd met under different circumstances. He would've had her splayed naked on his bed without a second thought.

Standing, he quickly pushed the thoughts from his mind. There was much at hand he had yet to deal with. His father would be arriving at the estate shortly. The matter of the missing rune would be discussed and he would have to somehow reveal to him the activities of the night and his failure to learn more.

He marched toward the stainless-steel faucet and washed his hands. Then he moved to a cupboard and pulled a woven quilt from it and tossed it onto the back of the sofa in the corner. "You would be wise to rest. You will need your strength for we have another long night ahead."

He stood there for a few more seconds, his eyes draping her once again. She said nothing, only sat there watching him as if he'd brought the plague himself. He didn't consider his actions wrong, far from it. He was loyal to his family and would do whatever it took to reinstate the peace that they'd fought so long to obtain. And if that meant holding a deviant and sharp-tongued vixen against her will, then so be it. In fact, the experience might just be good for her. There were a few lessons she needed to learn in obedience. Quietly, he stalked toward the door and left the room, turning the lock in the keyhole.

Daniela waited until the sound of Nicholas's footsteps disappeared down the hall. She pushed herself up quickly and carefully slipped her pants back up, wincing slightly at the subsiding pain in her leg. The dried leaves he'd added to her dressing were certainly working quickly. She hadn't been too keen on having him help her, but now she was glad that she had. If she intended to escape she would need every bit of her speed and agility working for her. She snatched up the pouch of leaves from the first aid kit and stuffed it into her pocket. There was no telling how long the anesthesia would be effective. And if she intended to find the second rune before the day ended, the last thing she could afford was the distraction of pain.

Reaching into her shirt, she found the cold metal that was pressed against her left breast.

It was the key to Nicholas's motorcycle. Upon entering the kitchen she'd deliberately stumbled against him and had deftly picked his pocket. And when he'd reached into the cupboard for the first aid kit, she'd quickly hidden it. She hadn't been bold enough to attempt retrieving her phone from his back pocket for he would've surely guessed her intentions.

She limped toward the door and slipped two hairpins from her hair. If there was one thing Nicholas had forgotten it was that she was a thief. He'd stripped her of her gadgets and re-trieved his pocket knife, but she was innovative. A mere door couldn't confine her. Straightening the pins, she stuck them into the old-fashioned lock system. She'd never picked a lock quite this antique before, and it proved to be more than a challenge. Nevertheless, after several tries she heard a soft click.

Slowly, she turned the handle and peered out into the hall. She was free! She eased into the hall, listening for any sounds beneath the abated rainfall and was met with silence. She closed the door of the kitchen and made her way down the hallway, hoping to encounter a rear exit. She noted the wet boot prints on the tiled floor and knew that this was the way Nicholas had come.

Halfway down the hall another passage branched off to the right and so did the wet boot prints. She could see a set of double doors that were closed, but light seeped from beneath and the distinct sound of voices could be heard. Daniela paused. She was torn between the desire to leave and to learn more about the man who'd disrupted her life in only a few short hours. In the end her curiosity got the better of her and she moved forward.

Chapter 5

Nicholas leaned against the mantelpiece of the large fireplace, a tumbler of brandy in his hand. He studied the occupants of the elegant sitting room. Present were his parents, his older brother Simion, their cousin Andrew and the six elders of their clan.

Garbed in a burgundy brocade jacket, Lord Victor Drakon adjusted the ruffles at his wrist. "For centuries the secret of the runes has remained sacred within our clan. It confuses me how any among us would choose to rekindle an ancient and evil spirit that had nearly ushered us into extinction."

The many years of his life had done nothing to dissipate the force and vigor of Lord Victor's character. He remained the strong leader who had brought his clan through the dark ages. Nicholas had learned many lessons from his father and he held him in the highest regard.

Simion spoke. "It must be one of us, for few know of the runes. The question is why now? Why after the curse has been broken?"

"And why in secrecy," Nicholas added. "Every decision made within our clan has always been a mutual effort."

Lord Victor reclined against the high back of his chair. "The motive is unclear, but that is the least of our concerns. If my brother and his followers are awakened, we would be helpless to contain them."

Ciprian, an elder who'd fought in the great Cetatean war joined the debate. "But if the Rune of Cythe is safely hidden we should have no reason to worry. One is useless without the other."

"Not quite," said Lord Victor. "If the missing

stone is damaged or even tampered with it can initiate the awakening. This will only result in an undeterminable and most undesirable conclusion as the process will never be completed. Not without its sister stone."

Lady Amelia, Nicholas's mother, spoke then. "And what of the sorceress who cast the spell, Victor? The Ananovians have been dabbling in methods to achieve immortality for years. Can we not seek her help?" Garbed in a vintage evening gown, she was the image of grace and beauty; a woman devoted to her fold.

Lord Drakon shook his head. "Agatha is long dead. She was traditional and cared not to see this world to its end. We have no choice but to move the rune to a second location."

Andrew expressed his concern. "Victor, is this wise? The rune is safe. Move it now and you could jeopardize that."

Andrew and his family were the direct descendants of Lord Victor's cousin Demetrius, who had been spared the curse of the gargoyle as he'd been in another village during the time it was cast. Demetrius had led a normal life while assisting his damned kin in any way possible. His subsequent generations had taken up his staff, maintaining their loyalty even to the very hour the curse was broken.

"It is a chance we will have to take," Lord Victor told him. "If this thief or those who hired her learn the location of the rune, all will be lost."

At the mention of the thief, Nicholas suffered a moment of guilt. Strangely, he hadn't felt compelled to reveal Daniela's presence at the estate. And what was even more shocking was his motive. He was protecting her. Although more than a year had passed since the curse had been broken, there were still those among his clan who had yet to embrace the subtleties of humanity. If discovered, Daniela would be subjected to more than a grueling interrogation. Selfishly, he'd decided to retain the responsibility of learning everything she knew for himself.

"My lord," came the voice of one who'd thus far remained silent. "I fail to comprehend why all this effort is being placed on assuring your brother's continued imprisonment."

All eyes turned to the one called Stefan, who, as one of the older members of their clan, rivaled Victor in both age and wisdom. He was a recluse however, and it was his habit to oppose anything that would bring change. Those who knew a little more of him understood that his recessive nature was usually mistaken for arrogance. He rarely attended any gatherings, and if he did make the effort he kept to himself. In fact, he was the only member of their clan who had been absent the night the curse had been broken.

"How can we be sure that they, like us, have not become human?" Stefan continued. "It would be only fair to give them the chance at life as we have been given."

His comment fueled a series of whispers that quickly filled the room. Lord Victor raised a hand, propelling the occupants once again into silence. "You are correct, but we must also consider the possibility that because their souls are confined, they have remained unchanged. Sorcery is a complicated vector and we cannot facilitate the process of awakening them upon mere speculation."

"And so we should leave them to suffer for all eternity while we walk free? It is hardly fair that there are members of our clan who are unable to enjoy humanity. If they have been exempt then there must be another way to break the curse."

Lord Victor's countenance grew hard. Nicholas knew his father well; he listened to reason, but in the end expected his word to be final.

"And what do you propose?" Lord Victor asked. "That we scramble about for a solution while my brother and his followers tear through this country, destroying everything in their wake? Do you not think that I have considered everything you have just said? Unfortunately, something must be sacrificed in this situation."

Nicholas agreed wholeheartedly with his father's decision. They couldn't risk setting loose an opposition that as humans, they were no longer able to control. He knew that it wasn't an easy decision for his father as Gabriel was his own brother, but such were the burdens of a leader.

Already, Lord Victor had gone against the advice of the witch Agatha. She'd instructed him to destroy the statues—Gabriel and his followers turned permanently to stone—since she'd seen no hope for redemption in them. But Lord Victor hadn't been able to bring himself to do so. Instead, he'd ordered that the dungeon of Fagara Castle be sealed shut with a thick wall of stone. As time had passed the castle had been reduced to ruin, but the twelve statues remained sealed within the darkness. No, Lord Victor wouldn't bend to his emotion a second time.

The safety of his people and of others had to be placed above his own sentiment.

Silence ensued as those present waited. When Stefan held his tongue, Lord Victor stood slowly. "I would ask you all to govern your households with watchful eyes for there may be those among us whom we can no longer trust," he said pointedly. "We will end these proceedings here and resume our discussion on this matter once the Rune of Cythe has been safely transported to another location."

The elders nodded in compliance and, with respectful goodbyes, began to move out. Nicholas watched Stefan slip silently from the room. Pale gray eyes locked with his and for a fleeting second he sensed a troubled soul.

Simion moved to stand beside him. "It is not clear what motivates his objections, but I feel he is not to be trusted," he said.

"I agree," Nicholas said as he turned to face their father.

Lord Victor paused a foot away from them.

"You are perhaps correct, but without proof I want no accusations made. A man should not be condemned for appearances alone. What I would have you do is retrieve the Rune of Cythe as soon as possible," he said.

Andrew approached. "My lord, again I beg you to reconsider…"

"That is enough, Andrew," Lord Victor said impatiently. "I have made my decision and it is final. Where I will most appreciate your insight is with Stefan's activities. I want his every move watched."

Andrew inclined his head. "As you wish, my lord."

Lord Victor nodded his appreciation. "Thank you. Now, will you please leave us? There are a few matters I would prefer to discuss in private with my sons."

Andrew complied, and once he was gone, Lady Amelia eased the door shut.

"Victor," she said quietly. "I was of the opinion that you alone knew the location of the second rune."

Lord Victor sighed. "I fear that over the years I have visited the location many times. It would take only a clever assumption for one to guess where the Rune of Cythe is hidden. We cannot afford to wait for this to occur."

He glanced out the window. Nicholas followed his gaze. Through the cracks in the heavy velvet drapes the bleak dawn spilled in. Even after more than a year of being human again he'd still not grown accustomed to the beauty of the morning. It was to him as awe-inspiring as that first flake of winter snow to a young child.

"Unfortunately," Lord Victor began. "My health will not permit me to make the journey myself."

Simion fixed him with a worried look. "Are you ill, father?"

"I fear the weight of my true age has begun to descend upon me," he told them.

Lady Amelia moved toward him with his coat.

"Nonsense," she objected as she helped him into it. "Your father has been a little out of sorts lately, but he will recover."

Nicholas studied his father. "Have your symptoms been reminiscent of those we experienced during our transformations?"

Lord Drakon's eyes narrowed on him for a second before he shook his head. "Not at all. Why do you ask?"

Nicholas looked to his mother then back again. The last thing he wanted to do was give her cause for concern. She was very nurturing and would no doubt take whatever burdens they held upon her own shoulders.

"Of late I have been experiencing similar aches. They are fleeting, but unmistakable."

Simion studied him. "How long has this been occurring?" he asked.

"Nearly a month." The look on his brother's face told him that he wasn't alone in his suffering.

"I have had the same experiences," Simion

told him. "They come during the darkness, often staying for only a few minutes at a time."

Their father's heavy brows furrowed in a frown. "And during this time have you noticed any signs of a transformation?"

Nicholas and Simion shook their heads in unison, but it was Nicholas who spoke. "The pains are isolated. They are never accompanied by any of the other signs."

Their mother turned a look of concern on to them. "Victor, what could this mean?"

He looked pensive. "I do not understand it, but we will not trouble ourselves by drawing conclusions before more is known about the circumstances. I will consult a trusted Ananovian sorceress about this matter, but for now, my sons, I need you to retrieve the Rune of Cythe."

Simion nodded curtly. "Just name its location and it shall be done," he promised.

"It is hidden within the Bellu Cemetery in your grandfather's tomb. It rests near his heart, so the crypt must be opened."

Nicholas nodded slowly, understanding completely now why the burial site had remained more than sacred to his father. The remains had actually been excavated from the tomb at Fagara Castle in 1530, twenty years after his grandfather's death. Lord Philip Drakon, his grandfather, had remained human after the curse had been laid as he'd not been present at the castle. Nevertheless, he'd blamed himself for the ungodly fate that had befallen his family. He'd been the one to suggest Victor's betrothal to Lady Vivian as he'd been thinking more of the continued success of his lineage rather than the emotions of those involved. And thus, in misery he'd withdrawn to an isolated estate in the hills. It was there that he'd spent the remainder of his days, branding himself a failure and thankful only that his beloved wife hadn't lived to witness it all.

"I will retrieve the rune," Nicholas offered.

He checked his watch. The drive to the cemetery was no short one, but he had a few essential things to do before he left. First, he needed to learn everything he could about Daniela. Her phone remained within his possession and he had a few acquaintances in New York who would be able to acquire the information for him. He needed to know if Daniela was as oblivious as she'd made herself out to be, for when the sun set he would have one opportunity, one alone, to retrieve the rune.

Lady Amelia interrupted the silence. "Victor, perhaps it is time we be rid of the statues."

They awaited Lord Victor's response. Nicholas understood well the hold the statues held over his father. Despite the stony countenance Lord Victor presented to their clan members, he still held himself responsible for the actions of his younger brother—Gabriel—so many decades ago. He was also plagued by guilt for being forced to exact such an extreme punishment.

Lord Victor's head fell. "I believe that good can be reborn in all of us and I have lingering hope that such is true for Gabriel. Truthfully, since our family's curse was broken I have been consulting Ananovian warlocks about potentially awakening my brother and his followers. However, no spells have been cast as a resolution has yet to be reached."

Lord Victor exhaled quietly and his attention strayed to the window again. "We will secure the second rune and leave destroying the statues as our final resort."

Daniela eased her ear from the base of the tall crystal vase that she'd been using to eavesdrop on the conversation in the adjacent room. The majority of what had been discussed had made absolutely no sense to her; with all the talk about curses and witches, she felt safe to assume that the Drakon family was anything but ordinary. Nevertheless, she'd learned exactly what she needed to know: the location of the second rune stone.

She placed the vase on a nearby table and stuffed the dried bouquet of flowers back into it.

She'd heard Nicholas volunteer to bring the rune back, which meant she would have to hurry. She knew where to find the Bellu Cemetery, but she had no idea whose grave she would be looking for.

Silently, she crossed the room and eased the door open. She could only hope that Nicholas didn't realize that she was gone, at least not until she was far away from the estate.

She looked out into the hall and paused. A man stood just outside the door of the next room, apparently listening to the discussion within as she'd been. With his back to her, his face was indiscernible. But with his tall and broad frame, he could've very well been Nicholas's brother. Nevertheless, his identity and motive didn't concern her. Right now the sun was rising and she needed to get out of there. Cautiously, she slid out from behind the door and eased her way back up the hallway. She had a rune to find.

Chapter 6

The heavy gray clouds dipped low in the sky and she could hear the soft moan of thunder in the distance. A gust of wind caught the ends of Daniela's hair, whipping it about her face as she stood at the entrance of the Bellu Cemetery. The place was a morbid gathering of ancient tombstones and brittle rose bushes in a lonely parish that had seen too few visitors.

It had taken her nearly forty-five minutes to reach the burial site that was just outside the city of Bucharest. She'd taken Nicholas's motorcycle and made one single stop along the way and that had been to purchase a phone card and ask for directions at a service station. There she'd contacted Mai and asked her to cancel her cell phone account and completely wipe any information on her. She'd been careful not to mention the difficulty she'd encountered for two reasons: she didn't want Mai to worry and she'd had no time to explain everything. When the rune was in her possession and delivered, she would be on the first plane out of there. She needed to get this job done as delivering the second rune was possibly the only thing that would exonerate her from any involvement in the ambush at the monastery.

Daniela gripped the heavy iron gate and pushed. The rusting hinges resisted, filling the silence with its objecting wail as it was forced open. She advanced and scanned the area. There were hundreds of graves surrounding a stone pathway that branched off into several directions. She exhaled. She certainly had her work cut out for her.

Wasting no time, she began moving up the

path. She tried to ignore her pensive audience of black crows that were scattered among the trees. They gawked in silence, their dark eyes unflinching. It was all Daniela could do to focus on the graves. Thus far she knew that she was looking for a tomb, and judging by the wealth of the Drakon family, she was certain it would be adorned with something elaborate.

A pair of mausoleums became visible near a huge oak tree and she moved toward them. They were littered with damp leaves, their entrances partially concealed by overgrown bushes. She walked to the first and peered through the metal gate. A single stone coffin lay within. She looked at the name that had been engraved above the portal.

Joldea Seneslav 1904–1962, she read. This definitely wasn't the one. She moved on to the next and concluded the same. Thunder rumbled again and Daniela continued walking through the graves. She moved quickly, hoping to be done with her task and out of there before the rain started. She advanced another few feet then stopped. At the far corner of the cemetery she could make out large stone wings peeking through the trees. A more careful look revealed the stained walls of an aged mausoleum. She shot a glance about and deduced that it was by far one of the more intricate tombs present. She headed toward it.

The heavy metal door was an interesting design of a gothic cross and it was secured by an old iron lock. What she had assumed was an angel turned out to be a statue of a hideous gargoyle perched just above the entrance. Its wings were spread to full length while massive claws gripped a brass rod that was fastened to the wall. And just below the figure the name Lord Philip Drakon was etched into the stone. The sudden burst of exhilaration that filled her stomach was short-lived for she read the dates beneath it—*1434–1510.*

Her eyes narrowed in confusion as she made an attempt to recall the exact words of the conversation she'd overheard. She was almost certain that the one who lay within the tomb had been referred to as Nicholas's grandfather. But that wasn't possible, not with so many centuries between them.

She circled the tomb, inspecting the names of the other smaller mausoleums present, none of which bore the Drakon title. It seemed she had found the correct one, but had perhaps heard incorrectly, she deduced.

She returned to the brass door that sealed the entrance and studied the lock. She wouldn't waste her time attempting to pick it for the thing was as old as it was massive. No set of hairpins would be able to unlock it. She looked about for another alternative and her attention fell upon a thick slab of discolored brick that had once supported the base of a headstone. She quickly retrieved it and brought it down hard on the lock. The subsequent *boom* of the door being struck echoed throughout the cemetery, breaking the eerie silence, and her dismal audience took to the sky in a chaos of fluttering wings and startled screeches.

Daniela wasn't deterred. She struck the lock a second time, then again and again. The fourth time proved successful and the lock broke away. Panting, she threw the stone aside and pushed the door to the mausoleum open. Light spilled in from the outside, revealing a dark gray marble floor and a matching coffin. She entered, descending three short steps. A deathly chill enveloped her, penetrating her clothing and searing her skin. Her attention was drawn to the walls. They were etched with writing that was both foreign and indiscernible, even unlike the language of modern Romania.

She approached the coffin. It was draped in a length of threadbare cloth that had clearly once been beautiful. Golden threads crossed it, adding to the faded depiction of a crest. With careful reverence Daniela removed the covering and set it aside. Her heart raced, for in all her unsavory adventures she'd yet to see death.

This was no time for fear, she told herself and gripped the solid lid of the coffin and pushed. It didn't even budge. She hadn't really expected it to, either. After so many centuries of solitude the thing must've been sealed shut.

She tapped on the lid, confirming that it was indeed marble. There was only one way into that coffin. As much as she didn't want any part in desecrating the dead, she knew it had to be done. Her own life depended upon it. Quickly, she raced outside and returned with the large slab of stone she'd used earlier. Without giving her conscience time to intervene, she lifted it high and threw it down as hard as her muscles would permit. The heavy block struck the marble and clamored to the floor. A huge crack at the center of the lid was her only success. She was careful not to aim too high for she didn't want to risk smashing the rune. She picked up the stone again and repeated the act only this time the marble gave and a splintering hole appeared.

Grimacing at the stale odor that poured out, she began moving the slabs of marble that had broken off. She then pulled the stone out, revealing the flash of silver chainmail. It didn't take her long to realize that she was staring at the shattered midsection of Nicholas's ancestor. Closing her eyes tightly, she reached into the hole and up toward the chest.

Her fingers immediately encountered a tangled web of something unpleasant and she yanked her hand out. A chill of repulsion slithered up her spine and she quickly wiped her hand on the material of her shirt as if she could eradicate the feeling. Fondling remains was hardly an appealing job, but there was no other way.

Inhaling, she forced any thoughts of repugnance to the back of her mind and slipped her hand into the coffin a second time. Again her fingers laced through the tangling of substance, but she forced them higher. The man with whom Nicholas had been speaking had said that the rune lay near the heart of the deceased. She found the opening of the garment and slipped her fingers in. Immediately, she encountered hollowed ribs and the ancient coolness of death. Her fingers moved higher still, searching for the spot where his heart had once throbbed. The smoothness of stone grazed her fingers and she knew that she'd found the object she sought. Bound by a length of string, it had been draped about the neck of Nicholas's grandfather. She wound it about her hand and gave it a firm tug. The string snapped and she pulled it out.

The Rune of Cythe lay within her palm, entangled amidst a length of gray-streaked hair. She quickly stripped it clean and wiped her hand as before. Daniela took only a moment to look the item over before tying the string about her own neck. The rune fell between her breasts. With one regretful glance at the mess she'd made, she headed toward the exit.

Outside the riotous clouds had gained weight

and wind speed, engaging the drying leaves in a dance to seduce the rain to fall. Daniela shut the door of the mausoleum and paused again to gaze at the heavens. She'd have the remainder of the day to prepare for her meeting with Cradle. After the riot Nicholas had caused the night before she was sure a new drop-off location would be in order. But she would play along as if she knew nothing of the incident. And once the rune was safely out of her hands she'd return to start a new life for herself—an honest life.

A gush of wind passed through the trees, tormenting the branches overhead. It swirled along the stone pathway, kicking the dust with a vengeance. An object that appeared to be a heavy black cloak was caught within it. It tossed and turned, its sway smooth and unnatural.

With curiosity, Daniela watched it. Her instincts told her that she should leave, but she stood there, intrigued almost. An odd prickly sensation overtook her and her heart began to thump in her chest. Something wasn't right.

The material paused on the pathway, its rhythm undiminished as it swelled in both height and width. Then, to Daniela's disbelief, the figures of two women slowly emerged from beneath it. Clothed in black robes, they stood together with the wind tossing their curtains of beautiful long dark hair. They were identical in both face and form, and when they spoke their voices echoed in unison.

"Give us the rune." Their tongue was thickly Romanian.

Daniela forced herself out of the stupor she'd been ushered into. She didn't know what she was seeing, but that she would solve later. For now, the impending threat of the two who stood before her was quite apparent.

"The rune or you die!" they spoke again.

Daniela brought a foot down on a fallen branch and as it was propelled into the air she caught it. She swung it to her side and made ready for whatever they had to offer. Under no circumstances did she intend to part with the object in question.

Their eyes hardened on her and the woman to the left slowly drew a hand from beneath her robes. From her fingers she dangled a golden chain that was weighed by a small green crystal. Her long nails had been painted black to match the hue of her hooded eyes that looked on with malice. Her hand began to sway. The stone moved with it, swinging from left to right like the pendulum of a great clock.

Her twin reached into her robes and drew forth a long silver knife, then with slow strides she glided farther to the right. Separated now, the women began to chant in accord. Their words caught on the wind, lifting high to carry across the expanse of the cemetery.

Daniela slipped back a few steps, her grip tightening on the thick branch she held. It was taking every ounce of her resolve to maintain a level head. Life had hardened her in preparation for many situations, but never had she encountered anything quite like this. She had the uncanny feeling that she'd somehow crossed into a world that many had no idea even existed.

A loud squawk resounded in the air above her and she resisted the urge to find its source. Instead, she kept her gaze trained to the two women before her. The one who held the crystal had fallen into an apparent trance; her head dipped back and her lashes beat rapidly against the air. Yet her lips continued.

Another squawk and Daniela risked a glance to the trees overhead. She blinked once, then again. The branches were littered with crows. They shuffled restlessly like minions awaiting the command of their leader. She brought the branch up and with her legs braced for balance, she gripped it with both hands. Whatever was about to take place wasn't going to proceed without a fight.

The woman to the right raised her hand then, her blade pointed to Daniela. Their chanting intensified, growing fierce with each breath. Within the next instant, the infuriated cries of the fowls filled the air and the beat of their wings was thunderous as they took flight. They swooped and surged toward Daniela. Simultaneously, the woman who held the knife attacked with a shriek.

Daniela ducked and rolled, avoiding sure injury, but before she could stand, the birds set upon her. She swung her weapon with precision and skill, effectively keeping them at bay. Her assailant attacked again and a battle ensued. The other woman was in no way as skilled as she was, but with the crows obscuring her vision and picking at any part of her they were allowed access, the fight was hardly fair. Daniela however, was determined to make it out of there alive.

The woman came at her again, this time with a wide swing that was aimed for her throat. Daniela ducked and thrust a foot into her midsection. Her attacker gasped and stumbled, striking her twin. The other woman was jarred from her trance as she staggered backward. Instantaneously, the flock of crows scattered, their cries piercing the air as they retreated into the storm clouds overhead.

The twins recovered quickly and the one with the stone began a new chant. In her grasp the crystal swayed and was soon filled with luminous light. It was then that Daniela realized that whatever power she possessed was contained within the gem.

The woman holding the knife quickly regained Daniela's attention again when she attacked with a venomous hiss. Daniela tossed the branch aside and spun around with a high kick. The heel of her boot made contact and her attacker toppled to one side.

Daniela turned her attention to the twin holding the crystal. It was this woman she had more to worry about. With only the awareness that she needed to get the crystal away from her, she charged forward.

Taloned fingers raised and deftly blocked her attack. Ensnared within her biting grip, Daniela fought to tear the chain from about her fingers. In their struggle, they fell to the ground. Daniela remained fully aware of the threat that lurked at her back. She glanced quickly over her shoulder and confirmed that the second woman was recovering. Kneeling on all fours, she watched the proceedings as she crawled toward her misplaced weapon. A trail of blood oozed from her hard pale lips and her eyes seethed with rage.

Daniela managed to get her fingers around the golden chain and she pried the stone from her opponent's hand. The woman fought harder then, clawing at her even as Daniela shoved her away and raced toward the edge of the pathway, her intention to smash the crystal using one of the stones that had been discarded at the wayside.

She managed only a few steps before fingers enclosed about her ankle and she went sprawling to the ground. The wind was knocked from her, but she hastily rallied herself. She reached high above her head, her fingers struggling to reach a weighty stone that reclined in the grass. Her captor had begun clawing her way up and over her body and she kicked madly, anything to be free of her. The woman's accomplice had also retrieved her knife and was headed for them.

With new motivation, Daniela managed to pull herself forward and she snatched up the stone. Lifting it high, she positioned the crystal beneath it and brought it down hard. The sound of the gem shattering was surpassed only by the incensed wails of the two women. She could feel the grip slip from her legs and she quickly sat up, prepared to conclude this madness. But to her profound astonishment the women had evaporated, leaving their black cloaks to fall lifelessly to the ground. Harsh cries lingered long thereafter, hollow and dissipating as if emitted by the spirits themselves. Struggling for breath, Daniela cast a weary glance about the cemetery as she reached into her shirt and pulled out the rune. It remained on its length of string, undamaged and secure. She replaced it and hastily climbed to her feet. With one final glance about her she hurried toward the exit of the cemetery, eager to be away from the place.

Chapter 7

The old building that housed the bed-and-breakfast had been around since the late 1500s. It was nestled within the heart of Sighisoara, Transylvania; the believed birthplace of Vlad the Impaler. Daniela's room was at the very rear of the house and she'd crept in quietly through a back entrance, escaping any suspicion from the owner and his wife. She was, after all, sporting a few bruises and a bullet wound.

She reached above the simple wooden door frame and found the brass key she'd hidden there. She slipped it into the door and entered, relieved to finally be within the security of her own space. On the long motorcycle ride through the endless rain, she'd replayed all the events of the past several hours in her mind. Had it not been for the aches her body had sustained and the weighty stone that remained draped about her neck, she would've thought it all a dream. The things that had occurred were unimaginable. It was evident that Nicholas and perhaps his entire family were part of a subculture that far surpassed her comprehension.

She'd also had time to ponder the identities of the two women—or whatever they were—who had attacked her. She recalled Cradle's description of the women he'd given the first rune to. He'd described them as twins. Surely it wasn't a coincidence that she should encounter the very same. Something didn't add up, though. If they'd known that the rune was hidden within the cemetery why hadn't they gone after it before now? Why hire her to come all the way from the other side of the world just to steal it?

Daniela threw her door's dead bolt into place

and limped over to the double bed that dominated the simple room. Carefully, she eased onto the faded quilt and slipped off her pants. She'd left Nicholas's motorcycle hidden within some bushes about half a mile outside the city. She was certain that by this time he'd noted her absence and that of his vehicle. The police had no doubt already been alerted.

The walk to the bed-and-breakfast had been an unpleasant one. Even now the bullet wound in her thigh ached miserably. She pulled out the pouch of dried leaves that Nicholas had referred to as kava. Tonight she couldn't afford to display any signs of an injury, especially one that Cradle was bound to recognize.

She was about to remove the slightly blood-stained dressing when her open laptop chimed softly with an alert that she'd received a message. She leaned across the bed and switched on the monitor. It was Mai. The system they had set up enabled her to not only talk to, but also see Mai no matter where she was in the world.

Daniela engaged the window and Mai's image appeared.

"You're up late," Daniela greeted her. "How's the weather in New York?"

The instant she spoke Daniela realized that something was wrong. Mai sat there with her long, dark hair partially covering her face.

Daniela pulled her laptop closer. "What is it?" Already her heart had begun to pound. Luck hadn't been in her favor and she feared it had just deserted her completely.

Mai looked up then and her hair fell aside, revealing the dark bruise near her left eye. "Daniela, something's happened."

"Oh, my God," Daniela gasped. "Who did that to you?"

"Look, I don't know what happened last night, but some guys just showed up here and started asking questions. They knew that we'd been hired to steal the second rune and were accusing you of snitching to the police…"

The world about her began to spin. Mai's

words were lost in the ringing within her head and only one thought came to mind. She'd been recognized at the monastery. "Where's Elaina?" she asked, her trepidation rising.

"They had guns. There wasn't anything I could do…"

"Mai, where's my sister?" Daniela interrupted.

"They took her," she said with great remorse. "They said they will contact me to tell me where the rune must be delivered. We have one week, and if you fail they'll kill Elaina."

Mai's words echoed within her head, and as slow comprehension seeped in, her heart began to pound. Elaina had been kidnapped and she had seven days to take the rune to an unknown location…or her sister would die.

Mai wiped at her tears. "I'm so sorry, Daniela. There wasn't anything I could do."

Daniela remained silent, for her mind was far from conjuring words, let alone speaking them. It wasn't Mai's fault, but her own that her sister's life was now in danger. Agony rose within her and her nostrils flared as she fought back tears. Too long had she put off reforming her life and now her worst fear was realized. She knew the ways of the men who'd hired her. Even if she delivered the rune tonight, her life and that of her sister wouldn't be spared. They lived by a code that was deadly, but assured their continued business success. Strings were simply never left untied.

A single tear crept its way down her cheek, doing little justice to the emotions that ravaged her soul. This morning had taught her that the mystery surrounding the highly sought-after artifact was far greater than anything she could have imagined. There was just no simple way out of this. Yet, she had to do everything in her power to save Elaina. She didn't care about herself; she would sacrifice her own life if she had to as long as Elaina came out of this alive. She couldn't do it alone though. She needed information. She needed someone who knew just how deep the veins of this dark world ran and how its inhabitants behaved. She needed Nicholas Drakon's help.

High above the ground, perched on the branch of an ancient oak, Daniela perused the Drakon estate. She'd arrived at the mansion and had impatiently waited for the household to settle. The Drakon family had scattered in their luxury vehicles until only a dull glow had lit a window on the second floor. She hadn't been about to simply waltz into the estate and demand assistance. After what she'd encountered in the cemetery she wasn't sure what to expect from anyone. She'd come to see Nicholas and Nicholas alone, and so she'd simply waited with something far less than impatience.

For the past three hours she'd watched Nicholas beyond the half-closed drapes. He'd remained behind a desk, shuffling through a stack of papers. She'd never regained her binoculars, but from her vantage point, she could clearly see his large and beautiful torso, bare save for the wealth of dark hair that spilled over his shoulders.

He looked excruciatingly handsome, but Daniela had purposefully averted her gaze. The last thing she needed was to entertain any thoughts of appreciation for the man.

Finally, at 11:00 p.m. Nicholas had stood and disappeared out of sight. A moment later the light on the second floor had switched off, drowning the mansion in complete darkness. That had been thirty minutes ago. Daniela remained on her perch, watching the uneventful darkness. It was time.

She extended her arms outward and balanced her way across the limb. She'd already decided to enter through a set of glass doors that were adjacent to the window she'd seen Nicholas in. Once inside it would be a simple task to confront Nicholas while he slept in his bed. She leaped from the branch and gripped the edge of the stone balcony, then with little effort she pulled herself up and over it.

Daniela moved near the door. Hearing nothing on the other side, she took the small knife from her back pocket and carefully slipped it between the narrow space that separated the doors. She spent only a moment manipulating the lock before it sprang free.

Gripping the handle, she eased one side open. Darkness lay within and her stomach began to churn. Her intent was to blackmail Nicholas, and she was sure that her efforts wouldn't be received graciously. It was obvious that he was a man who got what he wanted, when and how he wanted it. Withholding his family's heirloom from him in an attempt to gain his compliance was hardly a smart move, but she had no choice. She would do what she had to. Her only solace, however, was that she would have the element of surprise.

Slipping into the room, she closed the door quietly and pulled her small flashlight from her boot. She turned it on and swung it about the room, revealing an elegant display of medieval furniture. The light fell on the massive canopy bed and she realized a figure lay amidst the bedding. She moved quietly until she stood at the bed's edge.

She was allotted only a moment to ascertain that it was Nicholas before a muscled arm gripped her and she was snatched off her feet. The flashlight clattered to the floor and she found herself on the bed, face up with the cool edge of a blade at her throat.

Daniela's breathing was stifled as a heavy weight descended upon her. Gripped by fear, she remained completely motionless. The man above her traced the curve of her neck with what felt like the tip of his nose and he inhaled. His weight eased off her slightly and the knife slipped away.

His breath fanned the lobe of her ear when he spoke. "You risk much returning here," Nicholas said in a heavy voice. "For your own well-being you had better have the rune within your possession."

Daniela didn't respond immediately. She was gathering her scattered wits. She had to take control of the situation if she wanted to gain the help she so desperately needed.

"I do," she told him with more confidence than she felt. "And if you ever want to see it again you'd better tell me exactly what I need to know."

His breath lingered on her ear for a second longer, then he sat up. He leaned over her and light fell onto the bed. Daniela squinted against the glare of the Victorian lamp.

Nicholas remained above her, straddling her hips. Her effort to look away this time was futile. His image was stunning. He was lean; his muscled torso hard and chiseled. His dark mane of hair was piled at the top of his head in a disarrayed ponytail with stray locks spilling over him. His abdomen was even more impressive. Displayed were sleek and hard muscles and a trail of dark hair that dipped into low-slung satin pants.

A stack of papers fell to her chest, jolting her back to her predicament. She looked at them then at the man who'd just tossed them there. The look he gave her was hard and unforgiving. She imagined that by this time he'd discovered the mess she'd created of his ancestor's tomb. She picked up the papers and her pulse quickened. All of her pertinent information was displayed. It seemed that he'd managed to trace her cell phone before it had been deactivated.

As she perused the documents, she was bombarded by unpleasant memories of her life. She'd been born in Brazil. Her mother, Sarah, had moved to the tropical country after meeting Daniela's father, a Brazilian fisherman named Emanuel. Their marriage had been hasty and it wasn't until after a few months of matrimonial bliss that Sarah had realized her husband was an abusive alcoholic. Wanting her marriage to work, she'd stuck it out. Daniela was born, followed several years later by her little sister.

The abuse had become more violent as

Emanuel's drinking had escalated. Finally, unable to take much more, Sarah had packed up and left with her daughters. Returning to her life in the United States hadn't been easy. With no money and no real family to depend on, Sarah had been forced to work two jobs just to make ends meet. It was no wonder she'd fallen in love with the first man who'd offered her a better life. Only that life didn't involve children.

Daniela had been seventeen when she'd awakened to find her mother gone with only a note of apology and thirty dollars in her stead. From the note, Daniela had gathered that her mother had been so desperate for a new start and to be rid of any memory of Emanuel that she'd simply left. For many months after, Daniela had tried to find Sarah, but it had been to no avail. Daniela had known her father's address in Brazil at the time, but had refrained from contacting him. A life of abuse was hardly the future she'd wanted for herself and her sister. And so she resolved to make it on her own.

Nicholas's voice brought her back to the present. "Perhaps I should simply contact the authorities," he threatened.

Hoping to appear aloof, Daniela set the documents aside. "If you do, your precious rune will be lost forever. If you help me I'll return it to you."

She waited, hoping he'd realized this was the only way to regain his family's possession. His eyes combed her body, paying close attention to the many pockets of the hunter-green cargo pants she'd changed into. After the little strip search Nicholas had administered the night before, she hadn't been so foolish as to bring the rune into the estate with her. Instead, she'd hidden it within the forest outside of Sighisoara; buried it in earth with a massive stone as its marker.

Nicholas slipped the knife back into its sheath. "And what, dare I ask, would you require help with? Reforming yourself?"

She'd nearly forgotten how rude he could be,

but she wasn't aspiring for his approval nor did she care for it. She needed his help to find her sister and that was all. "If you don't mind removing yourself I will tell you."

His dark eyes narrowed on her, but he slowly eased from her body. He stood at the foot of his bed and waited with his arms folded.

Happy to put some distance between them, Daniela sat up and slid to the floor at the opposite end of the four-poster. "Apparently I was recognized at the monastery last night. My accomplice was attacked and my sister was kidnapped." She inhaled as she made an effort to throttle the emotion that was rising within her. "The buyers want the rune in exchange for her life."

From beneath his heavy lashes, Nicholas watched her quietly. The expression on his face was almost impassive. Daniela's stomach began to churn again. She knew nothing of the runes or their worth. Perhaps for Nicholas, their value was only sentimental. If he decided that retrieving the ancient stones was simply not worth getting involved, then her back would be against the wall.

With the intent to bring more than her own crisis into the matter, she continued as she bent and retrieved her flashlight. "I was also attacked at the cemetery."

This got Nicholas's attention. "Attacked by whom?" he asked.

"Two women. They resembled the pair that Cradle had described to us, only..." She paused, realizing just how false her claim would sound. "You wouldn't believe it if I told you."

"Try me," he said.

Daniela hesitated, but continued. "They appeared out of the darkness as if they were some sort of ghosts. They confronted me and demanded that I give them the rune, and when I didn't one of them sent a flock of crows after me. It was as if she was controlling them. I know this sounds ridiculous, but..."

"You say she commanded the crows?"

She nodded. "Yes, while her twin tried to poke holes in me with a knife."

He looked pensive, his eyes narrowed as he studied her. It was hard to discern whether he believed her or not.

"How did you escape them?" he asked.

"The one who'd summoned the crows had a crystal in her hand. It seemed that her power revolved around it. I managed to get it away from her and I destroyed it. And believe it or not, they disappeared."

She waited for his sarcasm, but was surprised when a contemplative look crossed his face. It was as if he'd absorbed her extraordinary tale without question.

"Describe this crystal," he said.

Daniela focused on the glare of the lamp and made an attempt to recall the details. As she'd been fighting for her life, the specifics of the gem had hardly been on the top of her list of interests. "It was attached to a chain and she dangled it from her wrist," she supplied. "It was green and had an odd glow about it."

Nicholas's arms fell away from his chest and he moved a few steps toward her. "Did she speak when using the crystal?"

Again Daniela nodded. "They were both muttering some kind of Romanian chant."

He nodded slowly. "I will assist you, but we will do this my way."

The look she gave him was far from agreement. "We tried it your way before and look what happened."

"I am not to blame for your inability to follow orders or your negligence to properly cover your trail. We do this my way or not at all," he said stubbornly.

Daniela gritted her teeth. It was useless arguing with him. "Fine," she agreed. "But if I don't approve of something I will speak up and you will listen."

His eyelids lowered slightly and he watched her for a few seconds. She held his gaze, knowing full well that she would need to establish her ground now if it was to be effective later. Finally, he turned and stalked toward a tall wardrobe and swung the doors open. He pulled a shirt out.

"Those you encountered tonight are witches of the Raba clan," he informed.

Daniela's brows drew into a slow frown. "Witches? Like pointy hats and broomsticks?"

The speculation in her tone was drowned by the breath-snatching shock she experienced as Nicholas slipped out of his satin pajama pants. They glided to the floor, revealing the entirety of his tall and very muscled body. A huge tattoo of a black dragon spanned the width of his shoulders, its tail tapering down his spine and forcing her attention to his very firm backside. Daniela nearly choked on the lump she swallowed and her gaze snapped away. Had he no shame? Something indiscernible fluttered within her, but she quickly dismissed it.

"No," came his response. "Witches like those

who would sell their own souls and that of their spawn if only to glean a profit."

She could hear him shuffling into his clothing. In her mind she was trying to rationalize what he was saying. There was hardly a reason for her to doubt his revelation. After all, she'd witnessed the entire thing firsthand. What other explanation could there possibly be for what she'd experienced?

Nicholas continued speaking. "They are a gypsy clan—wild and lawless, and are loyal only to those with the fattest purses."

"So they were hired like me?"

"Yes." The heavy thud of his boots moved toward her. "Someone has made an extensive effort to cover his trail."

She looked at him then. He wore a fitted black pullover and jeans. His steps took him to another tall closet. He threw the doors open and a light flickered on, revealing a collection of weapons. He pulled out a strap and slipped his arms into it. It resembled a gun holster, but two curved blades were contained on either side.

Daniela eyed him with both caution and curiosity. What sort of man, aristocrat or not, kept weapons in his bedroom? He was more than a collector, she was sure. It wasn't hard to recognize his familiarity with his weapons. He handled them as one who practiced daily and who knew how to wield them with deadly force.

He shrugged into a leather jacket, leaving it to gape in the front. "Where were you instructed to deliver the rune?" he asked as he pulled a knife from the closet and slipped it into his right boot.

Daniela shook her head. "I don't know yet. I was given seven days. I was instructed to wait to learn the location of the drop-off. But I can't wait for that. Something tells me that my sister and I won't just be allowed to walk out of there once I hand over the rune."

"You are correct," he agreed. "But there is much we need to learn before we even consider attempting to rescue your sister." He marched toward the door.

"Where are we going?"

"To the city of Tiraghol. The majority of the Bara witch clan resides there. I would imagine that word about the rune has moved among them."

Daniela matched his stride as he headed down the lavish hall and toward a set of staircases. "Do you think they'll just volunteer the information? They didn't seem like a very hospitable bunch."

"As I've said, they can be bought for any price. It should not be difficult to purchase their assistance."

At the bottom of the staircase Nicholas took a right and headed down a hall. At the end of it a door opened into what appeared to be a large showroom. On display, were about eight luxury sports cars and SUVs. She experienced a tinge of resentment as she was reminded of just how wealthy the Drakon family was. With so much at his disposal it was no wonder Nicholas behaved the way he did. He was clearly an indulged brat who'd just happened to attain maturity in one of the most beautiful bodies she'd ever seen. Not that she'd seen that many.

He slipped a key from a collection that was hanging on the wall then headed toward a very sleek and polished silver Lamborghini. A soft humming caught her attention as the Diablo's doors swung upright.

When he looked at her again a warning resonated in his eyes. "If you have been untruthful in any way, now is your final opportunity to admit to it. Going into Tiraghol is not the most pleasant of ventures. If I learn that you have been dishonest there will be repercussions."

"Do you think I could make something like this up?"

He shrugged then slid into the driver's seat. Daniela circled the car and entered through the passenger's side. The doors eased down and Nicholas turned the key in the ignition. Simultaneously, the garage door began to lift.

"You have been warned," he told her just as he placed the vehicle in Reverse and sped out into the night.

Chapter 8

Nicholas slowed his Lamborghini to a crawl until it was partially concealed by the overhanging branches that skirted the hillside. He threw the transmission into Park then reached beneath the seat to retrieve his semiautomatic handgun. He assured that it was loaded then tucked it behind him in the waist of his jeans.

Thirty years had passed since he'd last been to Tiraghol and he was hardly excited about returning. Often referred to as the Crown of Hades, it had been fashioned into the hills in the mid-1400s and dipped deep into the earth. It was unique, the only creation like it in the world, but accessible from various hidden entry points. An intended sanctuary, it provided refuge to witches and warlocks who cared not to engage in the modern world. Its inhabitants generally stayed within the confines of the gates. There were those however, who didn't always conform to the rules. Misdeeds were frequent and danger lurked within every shadow. For Nicholas, entering would be an even bigger risk for him now. He was no longer a gargoyle, so was therefore unacceptable; mere mortals weren't permitted beyond its gates and if discovered, by law, were considered fair game.

"I don't see anything."

Nicholas cast the woman in the passenger seat a look. She was really proving to be more trouble than he'd anticipated. The ruin she'd left in his grandfather's tomb could be described as nothing less than a desecration and now she was blackmailing him to find her sibling. Of course, he'd agreed to her demands for it was of the utmost importance that he learned who was behind the missing rune. At this point, he was absolutely certain that the transgressor was a member of the Drakon clan. One who was prepared to do whatever it took, including hiring witches, to obtain what he wanted.

Again Daniela assessed the backdrop of shadowy hills. "There's nothing out here. Where's the city?" she asked suspiciously.

His gaze roamed the land, finding the barren apple tree. It sat upon a low rise, marking the entrance to Tiraghol.

"The tree shrouds the main entrance. The city lies beneath the ground," he told her as he opened the door and stepped out of the car.

Daniela followed suit. "Is it one of those ancient cities? And why would anyone choose to live down there?"

"It is hundreds of years old and accommodates many. It is by choice that they remain." He closed the door. "You will stay here," he told her.

From the other side of the car, Daniela frowned

at him. "Like hell I will! My little sister could very well be down there, and you expect me to sit and wait? I don't think so."

He pinned her with a steadfast look. "I do not need the distraction of keeping you alive. Tiraghol is no place for you."

Her mouth fell open, drawing his attention to her full lips. "Excuse me? Keeping me alive?" she reiterated. "And what the hell gives you the idea that I need you to keep me alive?"

"Your display at the monastery was sufficient," he said flatly.

Her expression hardened. "I see you're forgetting how we got into that situation. I won't apologize for being desperate."

Nicholas watched her for a few seconds. He wondered whatever happened to the days when women knew their place. "And I will not apologize for refusing to allow you to accompany me. You will remain here."

They engaged in a silent battle of wills. It stretched over a full minute before Daniela, in an obvious huff, returned to the vehicle and yanked the door closed.

Nicholas looked at her through the driver's side. "Stay within the car. Lock yourself in. If anyone approaches, you will find a weapon beneath your seat."

She didn't respond; didn't even look at him in fact. She sat there, glaring out the windshield. Her ripe and beautiful chest heaved slightly as if making an effort to calm herself. Nicholas suppressed a smile. It was quite obvious that she wasn't accustomed to taking orders of any kind. With this amusing thought, he closed the door and headed toward the shadowy portal that led into Tiraghol.

That arrogant bastard, Daniela fumed. Through the rearview mirror she watched Nicholas disappear over a hill. He had some nerve insinuating that she was incompetent. She, after all, was the one who'd managed to steal two runes from him. And what the hell had he meant about Tiraghol not being a place for her? Was he also sexist?

She reached beneath her seat and her fingers encountered a sleek, cool metal box. Slowly, she removed the semiautomatic handgun and examined it. She'd never used a gun before and her experience with one was quite limited. Briefly, she and Mai had toyed with the idea of adding guns to their arsenal. They'd trained a few times, but in the end had decided against it. Guns were simply too dangerous. However, in this case she didn't have a choice. She checked to see if it was loaded then slipped it into one of the large pockets of her cargo pants. Two magazines of ammunition sat on the bottom of the box and she grabbed them and stuffed them into her other pocket.

She opened the passenger door of the Lamborghini and stepped out. If Nicholas thought for one moment that she was simply going to sit by and wait while her sister's life was in danger, then he was gravely wrong. She was prepared to do whatever it took to find Elaina and bring her back safely. And if that meant battling a few more crystal-dangling witches, then so be it.

She slammed the door shut and headed the way he'd gone. The ground was wet and muddy; not very conducive to trampling around over hills. She slipped a few times, but regained her balance before hitting the earth. Finally, she came to stand beneath the apple tree that Nicholas had referred to. It was a great and disastrous image: tall and leafless and leaning precariously to the left. Its massive roots wove into the earth and resurfaced to dangle over a dark hollow that was formed into the hill beneath it.

Daniela paused as she tried to rein in her scattering courage. She thought of Elaina. Her sister was relying on her. She was the only one who could save her. Reaching into her pocket, she removed the handgun before slipping past the curtain of vines. The passage was dark and damp and smelled of dirt. She listened, hearing nothing except the frantic beating of her heart. With careful steps, she began to advance over the uneven ground. The passage narrowed and angled left and she could see the soft flicker of light teasing the corner.

A torch was fastened to the wall of the new passage. Relentlessly, she moved forward. Her free hand was used to guide her along the walls and she soon found herself moving over an even floor. The passage began to slope downward and she leaned slightly backward to maintain her balance. It wasn't long before another portal appeared. Only this one was an archway that was filled with a hazy glow. Daniela continued her descent until she stood before it.

She cocked the gun before entering. She was greeted by a scene that would've never been expected in the world she knew. Before her a flight of wide stone steps descended onto cobbled streets. Houses that resembled those of the Victorian era lined both sides of the street. The place seemed deserted. It was still and silent with only the fog to move about the shadows. Dust plastered the glass windows and covered the dilapidated carriages that had been carelessly pulled along the sidewalks.

Slowly, she descended the steps and her attention was drawn to the activity above. She knew that she remained beneath the earth, yet a sky of thick and luminous vapor swirled above her. Its silvery glow lit the atmosphere, giving the impression of a daunting midnight sky. She immediately concluded that it was the work of witchcraft. After what she'd seen that day she had no doubt about what these Raba witches were capable of.

Exhaling a breath, she randomly turned left as there was still no indication as to which direction Nicholas had taken. She headed down the sidewalk, casting cautious glances at the houses as they loomed in their dirt yards. A broken sign creaked as it swung indolently, and from somewhere atop a withered tree a crow squawked. Daniela hastened her steps.

It wasn't long before she came to a fork in the road. As the others before it, it rendered nothing save an eerie stillness. She was in the process of choosing a direction to take when to her surprise a cloaked form emerged from one of the buildings on the right. Daniela quickly retreated back a few steps, concealing herself behind the paint-chipped wall of a house. From her place of concealment, she watched the figure move up the street. Its sex was indiscernible, but from the stride, Daniela deduced that it was female. Something glinted in the woman's hand, and Daniela remembered the way the witch in the cemetery had held the crystal.

Without a second thought she began to follow, keeping a safe distance behind. If the woman was indeed a Raba witch then she was sure to know where Elaina was being kept. Daniela's fingers flexed on the gun; she was prepared to do anything she needed to do to find her sister.

The figure crossed the street and headed for a wooden bridge that stretched over a wide chasm. On the other side Daniela could see the mammoth shadow of a windmill. It churned slowly as it sliced through the fog that rose from the gaping split in earth. Carefully, she moved over the rotting wood, allowing herself a single glance over the side. The bottom of the chasm was obscured by darkness, but the sound of running water could be heard.

The figure kept her pace. Quietly, and without suspicion, she slid along the bridge then angled to the left. The buildings here were fashioned from metal and apparently had been built with no specific plan in mind. They were cloaked in rust and branched into odd directions as if rooms had been added out of necessity rather than design.

The woman pushed one of the makeshift doors open a crack and slipped inside. Daniela jogged a few paces to catch up then peered in. The walls were streaked with corrosion and an orange light danced over them. Daniela assumed that a fire was lit somewhere inside. The hooded figure had come to a stop on a wide metal catwalk that had been suspended over a two-story drop. She stood motionless and with her back facing the door.

Daniela gripped the gun with both hands and eased inside. Her feet moved forward, one in front of the other as she advanced. She was about to lift her weapon when a raspy voice came from the woman before her.

"Why you follow me?" she asked.

Daniela stopped abruptly. She waited, and when the woman failed to move, she spoke. "I'm looking for two women who attacked me earlier today."

Slowly, the woman turned to face her. She was young, no more than thirty, and her face was smudged with dirt. She cocked her head to one side and long, tangled braids spilled from her cloak. She was hardly dressed like the witches from the cemetery. She wore a dirty white tank top, a short flared skirt, torn mesh stockings, heavy boots and odd trinkets that dangled from a belt worn low around her hips. What Daniela had originally thought was a crystal in her hands, was actually a set of bent silver forks.

The woman noticed Daniela's attention on the items and with a suspicious look, she quickly slipped them into a bulging pouch that was slung over her shoulder. "You…attacked…in Tiraghol?" she asked, and keeping her head low, she moved a little closer.

Daniela held her position, poised and with the gun held firmly at her side. The woman seemed ordinary enough, yet there was something about her that gave Daniela the impression she was far from normal. She wasn't sure if it was the peculiar way the woman cocked her head from side to side, or the way her eyes dipped over her, or her apparent lack of a vocabulary. Whatever it was, it was definitely unnerving.

"No," Daniela responded. "I was attacked in a cemetery."

From the corner of her eye she watched as the woman began to circle her, moving close to examine her clothing. Daniela didn't move, but her muscles tensed.

The woman sniffed her once, then again. "You attacked on surface?"

"Yes." Daniela's head turned to the right as the hooded figure came around to face her as before.

The woman sniffed her again and her brows pulled together. "You human?"

Daniela regarded her incredulously. "Yes, I would like to think so," she responded with a hint of sarcasm.

The woman eased back a few steps and a yellow-toothed grin leaped to her face. "Human," she reiterated with something bordering on exhilaration.

Daniela frowned at her. Something was definitely not right. Before she could even decide what her next move would be, the woman threw her head back and emitted a chilling cry. It was shrill and unnatural and reminded her of the squawk of a bird.

"Human," she said again as she inched back a few more steps.

Daniela raised the gun. "Don't move," she told her. "You're going to tell me exactly what you know about the Raba witch clan."

Laughter erupted in the other woman's throat. It lasted only a few seconds before she sobered. She glared at Daniela, her eyes dark and hungry. Daniela cocked the gun. The small sound echoed throughout the building, but it was soon followed by another sound. It was the clanking of metal. It started off slow then built into a feverous clamor as if something wild was approaching.

Daniela glanced about. The sounds seemed to come from all directions. She backed up. It was obvious that she wasn't going to get any information out of the woman. And she definitely didn't want to face whatever lurked in the darkness. The wise thing to do was leave. She began moving backward toward the exit.

A sudden noise sounded behind her and she

spun around, aiming her gun at the figure that had come to land a few feet away from her. The man straightened. He was tall and also dressed in layers of dirty clothing. She wasn't given the chance to react, for a moment later, six others joined them.

Daniela spun in a circle, her weapon finding each new face. The way they watched her was a clear indication that there would be no easy route of escape for her. She inched backward until she felt the cold metal side rail of the catwalk pressed against her lower back. She wondered if she'd just stumbled into a den of witches. Perhaps the very ones she sought. The clanking of chains echoed about them and the group parted. From the other side of the metal catwalk, Daniela could see a figure moving in the dark. It passed into the flickering light of the fire that burned in a nearby metal drum. What was revealed was shocking. The hulking figure of a man emerged. He was shirtless and covered in tattoos and his long hair fell to his waist in a tangled chaos. Eight large metal rings had been embedded into his chest and abdomen, and from each a chain was fastened. Six of them dangled free, but the remaining two reached behind him and were attached to rusting collars that clung to the necks of two women. Topless and covered in grime, they gripped at the collars, fighting to stay on their feet as he advanced.

Daniela swung the weapon to him, but glanced cautiously to those about her. She also met the imploring stares of the two women on the floor. In the recesses of her mind, she wondered who they were and how they'd come to be enslaved.

The hulking beast of a man inhaled deeply as he assessed her. "You bold to enter Tiraghol," he told her. "But more foolish."

It was all Daniela could do to hold the gun steady. She wasn't about to show any fear. Her survival, she was certain, depended heavily upon the decisions she made within the next few minutes.

"I'm looking for someone," she told him. "And if you can't help me, I'm going to leave."

She dared to take a step toward the door, but three of the men moved to block the portal.

"Stay as you are," the leader warned.

One of the women at his feet motioned wildly for her to leave. "Run!" she screamed, her face streaked with tears. "Save yourself!" Her outburst earned her a deafening slap that sent her sprawling to the floor.

"Human slut!" her master growled.

A pulsing anger shot through Daniela and she wasted only a moment before she took heed of the warning she'd been issued. As if on its own accord, her finger squeezed on the trigger. The loud bang that ensued reverberated about the chamber and as the bullet flew, Daniela gripped the metal side rail and propelled herself over it with fluid grace.

The incensed roar that echoed behind her told her that she'd not missed her target. She landed hard in ankle-high water that reeked like sewage. She scrambled to her feet, simultaneously slipping her flashlight from her pocket. It flickered on just as she raced down a pathway bathed in darkness. The small light revealed a narrow hallway with a metal stairway at the very end.

Amidst her own splashing retreat, she could hear the sounds of her attackers falling into the water then chasing after her. The racing of her heart matched that of her feet and Daniela suddenly understood exactly why Nicholas had forbidden her to enter the city. The place was dark and evil. Yet, if there was a chance that Elaina was being held here, her decision would've remained the same.

A series of loud cries sounded behind her and Daniela hurried up the metal stairs. She gripped the handle of the door and to her dismay discovered that it was locked. Frantically, she tried the knob a few more times, but to no avail. The scrambling proceeded along the hallway and she turned the light just in time to see the form of one of the men appear at the bottom of the steps. He leered up at her, his face now distorted as if he was somehow being transformed.

Daniela gasped in disbelief and aimed the gun at him, firing off two rounds. He was struck once in the shoulder and fell backward into the water. The others quickly leaped over him and bounded up the stairs. Daniela turned the gun onto the door handle and squeezed the trigger. The knob flew off and she gripped the edges and swung it open. Not bothering to close it behind her, she fled across a narrow catwalk and came to a screeching halt. The catwalk ended in midair, dangling precariously from two unsteady beams.

Through the door, five creatures emerged. They were hardly like the individuals she'd left behind. Their skin had become ashen as if the life had been sapped from them, their eyes wide and sunken and their mouths gaping portals of hollowed darkness. Together they howled in chaotic unison. For the briefest moment, Daniela found herself drained of all ability to move. Never in her life had she seen such a thing. It was as if she'd stepped into a horror film, only she was starring in it. But she was determined to survive. A shaking hand brought the gun up and she fired two rounds.

Without waiting to see if she'd hit a target or not, she looked over the end of the catwalk. The bottom of the chasm wasn't visible and a chain-link fence stood on the other side of the eight-foot wide gap. Slipping the flashlight between her teeth she backed up and then ran, leaping off the edge. She closed the gap effortlessly and caught on to the fence. The clanking sounds of those who pursued her swelled behind her as she began climbing upward. The corroded wire bit into her hands, but she ignored it.

A look over her shoulder confirmed that the creatures were not at all deterred. The largest of the group raced forward and leapt into the air. Daniela continued climbing even as the entire fence was rocked by the added weight. From below, she could hear the creature scampering after her with unnatural speed. She swung her gun on him and fired. The bullet struck him in the left arm, but served only to entice his anger. With a blood-chilling cry, he clenched the fence and shook it, sending a rippling wave along the wiring.

Daniela screamed as her feet lost their balance and she found herself dangling by one hand. The flashlight fell from her mouth and was swallowed by the darkness below. With a mighty bound, the creature closed the distance between them and one large hand clamped about her neck. She was roughly yanked away from the fence and extended out into midair. Struggling madly, she fought to pry the thick fingers from about her neck, but it was useless. Her eyes met that of the beast and she knew that her death was certain if she didn't act soon.

At point-blank range she fired at the creature's skull, shattering it. His body went limp and he fell backward. She fell with him. Together they toppled for what seemed near thirty seconds until they struck the surface of chilling water.

Completely submerged beneath the dark depths, Daniela could hear the infuriated cries of the creatures who'd been left on the catwalk. The rattling of metal soon followed and she knew that they'd not given up their endeavor to apprehend her. She surged upward until her head broke the water's surface and sure enough, the creatures were descending the fence. Their eyes fixed to her and their mouths gaped with unnatural dexterity as they howled for vengeance.

She had to get out of the water, and fast! She scanned the area as her eyes adjusted to the new dimness. Something solid and fetid brushed against her arm and she spun around to face it. The decaying and apparently partially eaten body of a young woman floated before her. And it wasn't alone. The entire surface of the water was littered with corpses, all bobbing lazily to the peaceful symphony of death. A scream clawed its way up Daniela's throat, but was stifled by the tearful sob that nearly choked her.

Desperate now, she scanned the area a second time. To her right she could make out what appeared to be a platform that rested just above the surface of the water. Set into the wall behind it was a fairly large circle of dim light. She began swimming toward it, simultaneously praying that it was an exit.

The water rippled madly as the creatures sprang from the fence and landed with vibrant splashes. Daniela dared not look behind her. Instead, her strokes became harder and it wasn't long before she was able to grip the edge of the platform and pull herself out of the water. She'd managed to keep the gun with her and she turned it on the nearest of the beasts.

Click.

The gun was empty. She turned and raced toward the rear wall and to her exhilaration realized that the light she'd seen was indeed an exit. It could've been described as a length of piping that ran horizontally through the wall. It was wide enough for a large man to pass through and it rested on a metal rack so that a space was left along the top.

Quickly, she climbed into it and began crawling toward the other side. She could see the flickering and hear the crackling of a large fire and wafts of charred smoke circulated about her. Hope sprang within her chest for she knew that freedom could very well lie at the other end of the piping.

A howl filled the space around her and she cast a look behind her. A hulking shadow was outlined in the entrance. Daniela quickly rolled onto her back and reached inside her pocket for one of the gun magazines. The creature eased into the passage and began making its way toward her. She released the empty magazine from the gun and slammed the new one into place.

Meanwhile, the creature continued its advance. It had all but jammed itself inside the passage, and so it shuffled madly as it tried to squeeze its way toward her.

Daniela pointed the gun it toward the beast and fired off two rounds. The sound of the shots, coupled with the screeching of the creature, was deafening as it reverberated throughout the pipe.

The echo was still in the air when the sound of scampering above her could be heard. One of the creatures was making its way to the other end of the piping. Daniela knew that she couldn't allow it to reach there before she did. Even if she managed to kill the thing she would be trapped for there was no going back the way she came; once the other end was blocked there was no telling if she'd be able to dislodge the carcass.

She began crawling forward, and then as the scampering noise moved directly above her, she aimed the gun and fired. She was rewarded with a horrendous shriek.

Her dilemma wasn't over, for the thing hadn't

died. It began to drag itself along the pipe. To make matters worse the sound of more scampering could be heard. Daniela began crawling again.

The creatures moved swiftly and it wasn't long before she could hear them passing over her as before. Squeezing her eyes shut, she pulled on the trigger, unleashing four bullets one after the other. A cry resounded above her and she didn't wait to discern if any of the creatures had been killed. She raced toward the exit of the pipe and crawled out.

Struggling to her feet, she looked about quickly and discovered that she'd entered a large dirt pit. On both sides small fires burned, releasing blackened smoke into the open air. A metal stairway climbed the wall of the pit and led to the surface. She moved to run toward it, but an excruciating pain shot through the back of her head and blackness filled her vision. Her legs weakened and she collapsed into the dirt.

Beneath the high-pitched humming in her

head, she could hear the clanking of chains, coupled with heavy footfalls. Moaning, she rolled onto her side and as she blinked back the haze in her vision, she could see the hulking figure of the creature with the chains embedded into his chest. One of his chains dangled from his hands and she guessed that it was with this that he'd struck her. The two women remained at his feet, whimpering as if they'd witnessed this before.

Daniela searched the ground for the gun and spotted it about two feet away. She began dragging herself toward it, but got only a few inches before she was snatched off the ground. Face to face with the creature now, Daniela's life flashed before her eyes. So many things she could've done differently. Things she could change if she could go back, if only to save herself—if only to save Elaina.

Chapter 9

Nicholas slipped the pouch of gold coins from his pocket and placed it into the palm of the witch standing before him. Her greedy talons closed around it and she smiled.

"Is there anything else I may offer you?" she asked.

He brushed past her and headed for the arched doorway. "That will be all, thank you," he responded as he exited through the black beads that dangled within the portal.

His steps hastened as he took a left down the shadowy tunnel. The sounds of gunfire couldn't be mistaken, and he knew that something was gravely wrong. Modern weapons were rarely used in Tiraghol. Also, it seemed more than a coincidence that on the very night he'd left the troublesome thief on the outskirts of the city with a loaded gun, that there should be shots fired within the gates.

A few more shots rang out and he quickened his pace until he stood at the exit of the witches' lair. It was fashioned into the stone and overlooked the majority of the city. From where he stood he could see a great pit that was lit by many fires. Off to one side stood the figure of a tall man with several others at his feet. He bent and gripped the arms of one of the women and raised her roughly to her feet.

Nicholas realized that the woman was Daniela. Anger seeped through him and he reached behind his back and drew his gun. Simultaneously, he leapt down onto one of the flat steel rooftops of the makeshift houses and began racing toward the site. He ran without inhibition, jumping from roof to roof as he bridged the distance between them.

He should've known that Daniela wouldn't have taken his request for her to remain on the surface graciously. But he'd not intended to stay in Tiraghol for more than thirty minutes. And now, in less than that time, she'd managed to get herself captured by what appeared to be a band of shape-shifters.

From the edge of a rooftop, Nicholas cleared the remaining distance and threw himself into the pit. He landed in a roll and came upright with his gun aimed at the massive creature who held Daniela. As he'd suspected, they were shape-shifters; a primitive race of witches whose powers enabled them to morph into various forms. The three deformed entities who loitered in the background were perhaps only a few centuries old and thus unable to complete a full transformation. The one Nicholas opposed was no doubt the leader of them. He'd heard of the creature who kept his slaves chained to his body; the flesh-eating monstrosity who called himself Leviathan.

Nicholas's attention lifted to Daniela who was struggling to free herself. "Release her," he said with checked anger, drawing the attention of the beast.

His gaze remained upon her and their eyes met. Relief and fear were obvious on her face and something unusual tugged at his conscience, but he quickly dismissed it. Her own stubbornness had wrought these results.

Leviathan laughed, but his eyes were venomous. "Will not happen. I have room on my chains for another whore."

Nicholas cocked his gun. "The woman belongs to me. Release her or you will drown in your own blood."

The creature sobered and his face hardened. "She is mine. Perhaps now you will learn to keep a tighter rein on your sluts." As he spoke his head dipped and a thick, blackened tongue emerged to trace a path along Daniela's neck.

Nicholas's jaw tightened as he watched her struggle even harder to free herself. She was soaking wet and dirty as if this was hardly the prelude to her encounter with the creatures. A sweltering heat was making its way up along his spine and he fought to control the rage that was building within him. He didn't know what angered him most; knowing that Daniela had yet again placed them in an unsavory predicament, or seeing Leviathan's hands on her.

Advancing a few steps, Nicholas began to circle Leviathan. "I'll not warn you again. Release her to me or you will face your death."

"And what of the code? All in Tiraghol follow the code."

Nicholas wasn't oblivious to the codes that governed the city. In all its chaos there were laws that remained sacred and the book of codes was among them. Daniela was human. She'd been captured, and as a result she was the property of the shape-shifters.

It would be no difficult task to simply kill the

lot of them, for his aim with a gun was as pre-
cise as that with his crossbow. However he was
certain that they'd drawn the attention of many
citizens of Tiraghol. To have them bear witness
to his blatant discount of their laws wouldn't
be very wise. He and Daniela wouldn't make it
out alive. The only way to reclaim his right to
leave with her was to challenge Leviathan to a
battle of mortal combat. A feat that may prove
detrimental for him should the creatures detect
that he, despite his apparent familiarity, was indeed a human.

His attention strayed to Daniela once again.
She would be Leviathan's plaything until he got
bored with her, then she'd be eaten. Leaving her
behind wasn't an option. She looked so defense-
less, but that wasn't the reason why he would
challenge the creature, he told himself. Nor was
it due to the twisting that he felt swelling in his
abdomen once again. It was because she held
the rune. She'd hidden it and was the only one

who knew where it was. To lose her would be to lose the rune for eternity.

Slowly, Nicholas eased his finger off the trigger and held the gun up. He placed it on the ground then stripped his jacket off. Leviathan understood his intent immediately.

"This whore must be very worthy if you fight to reclaim her," he said as his eyes trailed the length of her. "I will enjoy feasting on her when your bones are stripped clean."

With that said, he lowered Daniela to the ground and shoved her toward the others, who immediately grabbed on to her. He then gripped the two chains that bound the women to him and with both hands, snapped them. The women were immediately set upon by the other shape-shifters, who dragged them out of the way. He then withdrew a long knife that had been strapped to his leg.

Nicholas pulled the two knives that were in his shoulder holster. In Tiraghol to fight to reclaim something was to fight to the death, which meant he had to kill Leviathan.

The beast attacked first, swinging the massive blade. Nicholas ducked, avoiding a sure decapitation. The battle had begun.

Despite being human now, Nicholas found that his speed had been retained. He'd not engaged in such a fight, mock or real, since the curse had been broken, but his skill hadn't diminished in the slightest. He swung his blades with dangerous precision, yet the beast remained quick and his strength was daunting. Nicholas struggled to avoid injury and several times he failed.

Leviathan thrust a foot in his abdomen and he stumbled backward in the dirt. The creature immediately set upon him and a violent struggle ensued. Nicholas lost his knives as he fought to keep Leviathan's weapon from puncturing his body. Gripping three of the chains that dangled from Leviathan's chest, he tore them away. The creature's agonizing roar filled his ears, momentarily deafening them.

Leviathan retracted, cradling his body where his flesh had been torn away. Blood trickled through his fingers and was gladly swallowed by the earth. Nicholas didn't hesitate to claim the upper hand. He rose to his feet and slammed a knee into Leviathan's head, sending the creature sprawling into the soil. The massive knife was also struck from his fingers.

Leviathan however, was resilient. Using the thick muscles of his legs, he sprang back onto his feet. His face was contorted with more than rage and his body began to morph. His head mutated into that of a giant sea serpent with pointed fangs barred in anger. Thick scales rose from his skin and a wavering and spiked dorsal fin pushed through his spine. He charged forward and gripped Nicholas in a painful tackle.

Faced with this new opponent now, Nicholas's confidence began to falter. He was beginning to doubt his ability to defeat the beast for already his body ached. It felt as if his joints were aflame and it was becoming increasingly difficult for him to avoid Leviathan's attacks.

A moment later, the creature snatched him up from the ground and, lifting him high, threw him effortlessly. Nicholas struck the wall of the pit and crumbled to the ground. A sharp pain shot through his spine, the intensity shaking him. Groaning, he managed to push himself to his knees. He turned his head to watch as Leviathan approached. His huge form paused a few feet away.

"A fool you are to challenge Leviathan," he spoke, his serpent's tongue lashing out. "Now you die."

Nicholas's teeth clenched as another sharp pain shot through him. It knifed up his spine to pause midback. He arched upward as he attempted to stifle the ache. He knew he had to stand, to fight, or his death would be inevitable, but he couldn't. The strength had been sapped from him and the pain he felt was too great.

A sudden ripping moved down his back and he cried out. He was certain that Leviathan had carved a slit in his flesh with the knife, but a glance to the side revealed that his opponent had paused in his advance. Leviathan stood there watching him with interest.

Nicholas moaned again as the ripping continued and he could hear the progressive ripping of his shirt. From his back, two massive wings sprang forth, initiating the transformation that hadn't taken place in over a year; the transformation that should not have been able to occur since the curse had been broken.

Two thick horns pressed through his skull and his face contorted as his teeth sharpened into fangs. His hair, already a thick mass, spilled over him to fall at his waist. His body expanded, growing taller and thicker with sleek muscles bulging and flexing with his every movement. He'd become a gargoyle.

Slowly, Nicholas climbed to his feet. His wings stretched to their full length of twelve feet, relishing their freedom after so long being dormant. He wasn't given the time to ponder how his transformation had come about, for Leviathan, realizing the new threat, attacked.

He charged, slamming Nicholas into the wall. Dirt crumbled about them and they went down in an earth-shaking tackle. With his transformation, Nicholas had gained both strength and speed which matched if not exceeded that of his opponent. But Leviathan was a skilled fighter—ruthless and savage, a callous beast who possessed no regard for any life save his own.

The battle waged. Nicholas broke free of the bruising death lock and took flight, somersaulting in the air and landing in a crouch on a metal beam that extended across the open pit. Leviathan stood and glared up at him. Blood dripped from the tips of one of his massive clawlike hands. He brought it to his face and his tongue snaked out, greedily licking away the fluid.

It was then that Nicholas realized that he was

injured. He stood and wound a fist into what remained of his shirt and tore it from his body. Three twelve-inch claw marks cut into his abdomen. Blood trickled from the wounds and they burned as if alight with flame. Nicholas's eyes slowly slid to Leviathan. He'd had his fill of this beast.

The heavy beating of his wings filled the silence as he sprang from the beam and swept toward Leviathan. Before his opponent could move, he slammed into him and gripped the remaining chains that dangled from his chest. As they met the ground together, Nicholas brought the chains about Leviathan's neck and used his body to pin him. He wound the chains tightly, pulling them until the sickening sound of bones snapping could be heard.

Leviathan thrashed about, his strangled voice crying out into the night as his body fluctuated between the forms of various creatures. Nicholas's hold didn't relent. The veins in his arm surfaced as he increased the pressure even

more. He never enjoyed killing, but this monstrosity was well-deserving of his end; his days
enslaving and raping women and devouring
their flesh had come to a fitting conclusion.

Nicholas watched as the light faded from
Leviathan's eyes. He maintained his hold for
another minute, needing to be certain the world
was free of this scourge. When the creature
remained still, Nicholas stood. Not sparing
Leviathan's body another look, he turned to the
two women who the creature had enslaved. The
other shape-shifters had begun withdrawing
back into the shadows. With their leader dead
now, they dared not challenge Nicholas.

"You are free now," he told the cowering fe-
males. "The gate lies to the north. Go quickly."
He pointed.

They hesitated only a moment before fleeing
in the direction he'd indicated.

Slowly, his attention moved to Daniela. She
sat in the dirt with wide fear-filled eyes as she

regarded him. He was hardly pleased that she'd just witnessed his transformation; something not even he understood. The complexity of the situation had just transcended anything he could've imagined when he'd agreed to comply with her demands. Now she was a liability. He didn't trust her, and the continued safety of his family and the secrets surrounding them was essential.

His chest heaved as he fought to steady both his breathing and the emotions that were raging within him. All this had been brought about because of her. Single-handedly she'd managed to disrupt the newfound peace he'd been enjoying. She'd stolen the rune stones, destroyed his grandfather's tomb and tonight, because of her stubbornness, she'd nearly gotten herself and him killed. Anger overtook him as he stalked toward her.

Daniela's heart drummed wildly in her chest as the beast that had once been Nicholas began moving in her direction. His face was masked in displeasure and his eyes were fixed to her with a determination that made her quake. She had the distinct feeling that she'd just been rescued from one danger only to be ushered into another.

With a whimper, she scrambled across the dirt and snatched up the fallen handgun. She staggered to her feet and raced toward the iron stairway that led out of the pit. Too much had occurred during this night. She was in no way ready for more. Her only thought was to get the hell out of there, away from the demons, away from the stench of death and away from Nicholas Drakon.

As she scampered up the steps she could hear the beating of massive wings behind her. A look over her shoulder confirmed that Nicholas had taken flight and was headed for her.

"Stay away from me!" she screamed as she climbed out of the pit.

She'd entered what appeared to be a junkyard.

It was littered with old and rusted cars, furniture and scrap metal. She wove her way through the mess and when a huge shadow fell over her, she spun around. Nicholas was descending to the ground a few feet away from her.

"Stay away or I'll—" Her threat was cut short when Nicholas closed the distance between them and, in one steel grip, brought her hands above her head. He snatched the gun from her and tossed it aside.

"Why is it so difficult for you to follow instructions?" he growled in a lethal voice.

His large body towered above her as he glared down with eyes that were both infuriated and chastising. She began to struggle, anything to get away from him. With a very impatient growl, Nicholas swung her around and brought her down flat on her back on the hood of an old sedan.

With her hands still pinned above her head, Daniela's body went rigid. In disbelief she assessed the creature he'd become. Gone was the beautiful man who could steal her breath with a simple glance. In his place was a tall and powerful entity; strong and domineering. The way his eyes roamed her body made her nipples peak beneath the wet material of her shirt. She didn't know what to expect for it was evident that with his form, his temperament had also swelled. And lord knew Nicholas had been enough to contend with before.

For a moment longer he watched her, then, with a moan, his head dipped and his mouth claimed hers. The warmth of his lips and the savagery with which he took her, created a mixture of fear and intense desire within her. A large hand moved to spread her legs and as he stepped between them, she trembled. Never had she been kissed this way. To her surprise her body began to respond. Her lips parted, welcoming his tongue.

Nicholas must've felt her surrender for his hold loosened but remained firm. With their bodies so close she could feel every powerful inch of him; thick and taut muscles flexing as he braced himself above her. And there was no mistaking the hard bulge in his trousers. Daniela dared not move for fear of inciting something within him that she was hardly prepared for. Instead, her eyes fluttered closed and she succumbed to the warm sensation that was consuming her.

At the recesses of her mind, she frantically questioned the sanity of her actions. Here she was, sprawled on the hood of a car and passionately making out with a man who possessed wings and horns. And to make matters worse, he'd just violently murdered another. Yet none of it seemed to matter. The taste of him was simply too intoxicating.

The kiss simmered to a sensuous ending and Nicholas withdrew from her. Daniela's eyes eased open and met his contemplative and accusing stare. Somehow he'd returned to himself. The creature had dissipated, leaving the man in its wake. He turned away and bowed his beautiful head as if he was ashamed of what he'd just done. As if kissing her was more vile than taking a life.

She sat up and slid from the hood of the sedan. She was shaking as her mind fought to come to grips with all that had taken place within the past hour.

Nicholas's head turned to the side and when he spoke the anger was gone from his voice. "If you care nothing for your own life at least have consideration for those of others before you act," he said quietly.

Without waiting for her response, he stalked toward his handgun, snatched it up and began heading in the direction of the gate.

Daniela stared after him for a few seconds. She had no choice but to follow Nicholas. He would see her safely out of Tiraghol and she needed him to find her sister. Yes, he was perhaps as deeply integrated in all this demonic madness as the creatures who'd attempted to capture her. But that she would have to over-look. He was her only hope, and with a shud-dering sigh, she reluctantly followed.

Chapter 10

The morning had come quickly. The smell of baking bread filled the air of the small tavern in the remote village of Viscri. Nicholas slipped outside and was met with the coolness of the dawn as he headed toward his Lamborghini. He'd rented a set of rooms over the tavern for the few hours that had remained before the sun rose. The ache in his body had subsided, but his wounds had needed tending.

Daniela had made use of the shared bath then she'd disappeared shortly after, presumably into her own bedroom. He hadn't bothered seeking her out for he knew she wouldn't go very far.

The events of the past day had escalated into something even she would be unable to face alone.

The drive to the village had been made in silence. His thoughts had been consumed by all that had just happened to him. He understood now that his transformation had been inevitable. Though he'd experienced the aches associated with the change for months, an inciting factor had eluded him. Until last night. There was also the question of how many of his clan had been affected. Thus far, only his brother had admitted to having experienced the same symptoms. Could there be a possibility that they'd been singled out?

Nicholas didn't expect to find answers in one night. He would go and consult his brother Simion. His parents would also have valuable insight, since in their endeavor to break the curse, they'd studied much about the art of witchcraft.

Opening the door of his car, he pulled out his

jacket and slipped it on, careful not to aggra-
vate the wounds on his abdomen that he'd just
rewrapped with bandages. Taking a quick look
about the area, he spotted Daniela huddled on
a rock and staring into the unwavering surface
of the lake.

He was immediately reminded of the way
she'd tasted on his lips. He'd been furious when
he'd discovered she'd placed herself in such danger; more inclined to throttle the little thief than
kiss her. And yet, as he'd gazed down at her,
something within him had turned to pure lust.

She'd looked so beautiful with her wet hair
framing her face. And her eyes had been wide
with fear, though unnecessarily so. The last
thing he'd want to do was harm her. Even now
he felt the sting of guilt for losing his temper
and treating her the way he had. It was understandable that she'd be willing to face any danger to rescue her sister, but if she wanted to do
so and come out of it alive, she'd have to learn
to obey him.

He headed in her direction. His brother's home was at least an hour away and he needed to get there before he passed out from exhaustion.

Daniela didn't look up when he approached, nor did she speak. He stood there for a moment, watching her.

"It is time to leave," he said quietly.

A few seconds elapsed before she stood. "Where are we going?" she asked.

"My brother's estate," he told her. "It has been a long night. We should leave as soon as possible."

She nodded. "Did you learn anything in Tiraghol? About my sister, I mean?"'

She'd been crying. Even in this twilight it was evident. Nicholas's head fell. He'd never been inclined to catering to softer emotions. He'd been wrought as a warrior; he fought, killed and suffered his woe in silence.

"Yes," he said honestly.

Hope washed over her face and he could see

her struggling to conceal her sadness. "What did they tell you?" she asked.

He had the unbelievable urge to reach out to her, but he resisted. "From the Raba witches I learned that one who calls himself Sabbath is after the rune. He was the one who hired you to steal the Rune of Moloch, and who hired the witches to find its partner stone."

"I guess they were hired after he learned that I'd betrayed them." She appeared confused. "But how did they know where to look?"

Nicholas had been pondering this very thing and had come to a conclusion; the one who called himself Sabbath was an elder of the Drakon clan. Only his own family and the elders had been present at the estate two nights ago. Had the true location of the Rune of Cythe been known before then, Daniela would've been instructed to go there instead of the castle.

He pinned her with a look. "How *did* you know the rune was in the cemetery?" he asked.

"I eavesdropped," she admitted with a hint of

embarrassment. "After I managed to get out of that room you'd locked…" She paused. "Wait. There was a man at the door. He was also listening to your conversation."

"A man?" Nicholas's brows furrowed.

"Yes. I was in the room next to the one you were in. And as I was about to leave, I saw a man in the hall. I couldn't see his face, but I could tell he was listening at the door."

Her admission sent waves of anger through him. He'd been right. It was bad enough to suspect that the traitor was one of his own clansmen, but to learn that it was one of the elders was sickening. They were the guardians, the watchmen, the decision makers of the Drakon clan. It was unbelievable that one of them would betray his own people. And to what end? Nothing good could be gained by awakening Gabriel and his followers. Nicholas's thoughts immediately fell on the only member who'd challenged his father's decision: Stefan.

He motioned to Daniela. "Come," he said as

he turned and headed in the direction of his vehicle.

He would contact Simion so that he'd expect their arrival. He'd taken a few steps when he realized that Daniela hadn't moved. He tossed her a look over his shoulder. She was just watching him, and the look in her eyes warned him of what was coming.

"Aren't you at least going to explain what happened back there?" she asked.

He turned away. "There are matters you do not need to concern yourself with."

He didn't have time for explanations, and besides, she'd been exposed to too much already. The less she knew the better, for both of their sakes.

It was obvious that Daniela didn't agree. "How can you say that after what happened last night? I was nearly killed by some body-morphing cannibal...."

"That was by your own doing," he interrupted. "You have no one to blame but yourself."

"That's beside the point," she countered. "I'm in this whether I want to be or not. I think it's only fair that I know what I've gotten myself into. I watched you change into some kind of bat for heaven's sake. I want to know what the hell is going on!"

Slowly he turned to face her. "It eludes me why you think you are entitled to an explanation. Everything that has happened was initiated by you."

He stepped closer, forcing her to tilt her head back to meet his stare, and the look she gave him was one of pure determination. His eyes narrowed on her. Her strength and courage intrigued him. There weren't many women who would have ventured as deep into Tiraghol as she had, not even to save their own child. And now here she stood, facing him with not even a flicker of fear in her eyes, even after she'd seen him release his inner dark creature.

"I agreed to help you find your sister in exchange for the rune and that is all. You would do well to forget everything you witnessed last night. There are things in this world you would never understand."

Her slender arms moved to cross over her chest. "Try me," she told him.

Nicholas recalled presenting her with that very challenge while in his bedroom. His attention dipped to her mouth. She stood there with a stubborn set to her jaw. Memory of the kiss they'd shared came back to taunt him.

"The sun rises. We need to leave," he said and moved towards the car.

"I'm not leaving here until you tell me exactly what happened to you back there," she told him. "If I'm going to trust you, I need to know who or what you are."

Nicholas released an impatient sigh as he was reminded why he'd sworn to an eternity of bachelorhood. He was really too exhausted to argue with her. If knowing more about the dark world his family had been propelled into was going to make her more compliant, then so be it. Of course, he wasn't comfortable with the idea, for there was the chance that after everything was settled, she'd go to the authorities. But without any substantial proof, her claims would seem bizarre and unrealistic.

"Very well," Nicholas said at last. "If you must know, over five hundred years ago my family was cursed by a witch. We were doomed to walk the earth not as men, but as gargoyles. The curse would endure as long as there were living descendents of the witch." He paused, awaiting her reaction.

"So you have been a gargoyle for five hundred years?"

He nodded. He could see her mind working as she absorbed what he'd told her.

"A year and a half ago," he continued. "My younger brother, Marius, was sent to New York." He paused as shame and regret began to move through him. "His mission had been to kill the last descendent of the witch, thereby breaking the curse. Instead, he fell in love with her."

He noted that a wary look had crept into her eyes at the mention of killing. Nevertheless, she remained attentive, permitting him to continue.

"Once we'd learned of Marius's transgression, our older brother and I sought to complete the task that Marius had neglected. But Marius opposed us and fought to save Alexandra. In a careless act that I will never forgive myself for, I accidentally killed my brother."

It was then that a look of shock crossed her face and her lips separated in a silent gasp. "You killed him?" she breathed.

Nicholas hung his head as images of that dreadful night slithered into his thoughts. Of all the things he'd faced in his life, he'd never been so afraid or broken as the moment he'd watched Marius collapse with the spear he'd thrown passing through his body.

He sighed. "At the moment of his death, the spirit of Alexandra's ancestor led her into chanting. In the end, it was Alexandra's love for

Marius and this ancient magic that broke the curse and returned my brother to life."

Daniela looked away briefly, her face a myriad of emotions. "But if this curse was broken, what happened to you tonight?"

"I am not certain. A few months past, I began having the aches that were always associated with my transformation, but I'd never expected this. My brother Simion has had similar experiences."

"So he's a gargoyle, too?"

He shook his head. "Again, I do not know. There is a possibility that we are the only ones in our family who will have to suffer this." He focused on the slivers of morning sunlight that had begun to stretch from beneath the horizon. "You see, when we realized that the curse was dissipating, Simion and I had deemed ourselves unworthy of emancipation from it. And so, in an act of contrition, we attempted to cast a barrier spell to avoid the magic. However, the incantation had been improperly performed and as the sun had risen, we'd become human."

Understanding was evident on Daniela's face. "So you believe that this barrier spell might've worked?" she asked.

He nodded with a grunt. That seemed a fair enough assumption, but even that was riddled with questions. If in fact the spell had worked, then why had it taken so long to manifest? Nearly two years had passed since that night. Something had to have occurred to either hinder the process or initiate it.

A frown creased Daniela's sleek brows as she looked at the horizon now ablaze with streaming shades of gold. "Wait, I just thought of something. Gargoyles turn to stone during the day. Or is that just the way the legend is written?"

"Your assumption is accurate," he told her. "Before last night that is how it has always been."

The myth of gargoyles, however, had been somewhat exaggerated. They were usually described as grotesque little nocturnal beings that were doomed to spend eternity guarding castles and holy places. Their fate was punishment for sins committed during another lifetime. These myths had been created by storytellers who'd taken eyewitness accounts and woven them into fanciful tales. One of the few facts that had remained true was that they did indeed become stone during the day. However, his transformation was no longer governed by day and night. It seemed he had complete command over it. He'd spent the majority of the early morning testing this theory. Several times he was able to transform by merely willing it. Becoming human again was just as simple. And with each transformation the agony seemed to lessen.

"And the runes," Daniela asked. "Why are they so important?"

Nicholas's eyes narrowed on her. As long as she held the Rune of Cythe he didn't think it was a good idea to reveal the true importance of the stone to her. She'd already proven that she'd do anything to get her sister back safely. He was sure that didn't exclude betraying him.

"They hold magical capabilities and are sacred in my family," he told her. "They have been within our possession for generations and their worth is unparalleled."

Whether Daniela believed him or not, he couldn't tell, but it was all the explanation she was going to get. He could feel the glow of the sun warming his back. It was time to leave.

"Come," he said again.

This time he didn't stop as he made his way back to his car. Too much had taken place this night and he had the foreboding suspicion that things would only get worse.

Chapter 11

Daniela glanced out the car window as they pulled into the mansion's gravel driveway. The place was elaborate and beautiful. With its neatly trimmed hedges, stone statues and rose bushes, it reminded her of a movie set.

The engine of the Lamborghini hummed off and Nicholas slipped the key from the ignition. She was still struggling to come to terms with all she'd experienced and learned over the past twenty-four hours. Since her arrival in Romania she'd been shot, taken hostage, attacked by witches and shape-shifters and kissed by a five-hundred-year-old gargoyle.

She shot Nicholas a quick look. She'd gathered that he had many layers to him, but never in her wildest imagination would she have guessed that the man beside wasn't a man at all, but a creature that she'd only read of in stories. Had she not witnessed his transformation for herself she would have never believed his admission. The entire ordeal for her had been both frightening and intriguing. What was even more confusing though, was that after everything she'd learned she still found herself very much attracted to him.

Nicholas zipped up his jacket, concealing the bloodstained bandages. "From this point on you will behave as if we are in a relationship," he told her.

"What?" she asked incredulously as his voice invaded her thoughts.

"My parents have been staying here while our main estate is undergoing renovations. If my father learns your true identity, and that you are withholding the rune, things could become quite interesting for you." The doors of the Lamborghini swung upright and he stepped out. "During your time here you will be considered my woman. And for your sake, make an effort not to steal anything."

With that he shut the car door and made his way up the stone steps that led to the huge double entryway. Daniela exited the car and followed. Her mind was racing. She really didn't appreciate his method of doing things, making all the decisions without consulting her and then expecting her to simply comply.

"Excuse me?" she asked when she met him at the door.

He was in the process of using one of the brass metal knockers. "Shall I reiterate?" There was no mistaking the sarcasm in his tone.

"No," she whispered angrily. "But you can explain the logic behind your ridiculous plan. Do we even need to be here?"

"We do, and the logic is you will remain

safe while we are here. I am not in the habit of bringing women to meet my family. The only plausible explanation would be to say that we are in a relationship that has progressed beyond a few nights of passion."

Daniela gasped, but before she could protest, the door swung open. The man who filled the expanse was tall, dark and very handsome. Instantly, she noticed the resemblance. He looked enough like Nicholas to be his brother, except the man before them was meticulously dressed in a suit and tie. He also sported a neatly trimmed goatee and a head of dark hair.

He stepped to one side and his gaze flitted from Nicholas to her and back again. "You certainly took your time getting here," he commented.

Nicholas placed an arm about her waist and ushered her into the foyer. "I was detained," he said.

The other man closed the door behind them. "So I see." Again his eyes trickled over her.

Daniela made an attempt to fight her discomfort. She'd never entered a house like this through the front door before, and she certainly felt out of place. Standing in the lavish room surrounded by marble tiles, expensive oil paintings and a crystal chandelier, she became acutely aware of her simple attire that was at present soiled and rumpled from her midnight excursion. Her hair was a mess, too. She'd washed it and it had dried slowly. Now it fell about her in a tangled mess of curls.

Nicholas's fingers remained on her lower back and it felt as if they were searing holes through her shirt. He looked at her and offered her a surprisingly gentle and reassuring smile. She was caught off guard and for a moment could do nothing but stare at him. He was so beautiful.

"Daniela, this is my brother Simion," he introduced. "Simion, Daniela and I have been dating for a few months."

She exchanged pleasant greetings with his brother, who didn't look thoroughly convinced.

A servant appeared from around the corner, rescuing them all from an uncomfortable silence.

"Shall I take your jacket, Master Nicholas?" he asked.

Nicholas shook his head. "No. I am fine, Emil. But allow me to introduce you to Lady Daniela. You can show her to one of the guest suites."

The servant nodded and politely motioned for her to follow. "This way, my lady."

Eager to get away, Daniela allowed the servant to lead her out of the room. It was odd being referred to and treated as a lady. She was certain she didn't look the part.

She was led up a wide staircase and down a hall. The entire mansion had a tasteful vintage appeal. She was hard-pressed to keep her attention from wandering over the gilded wall mirrors, velvet drapery and elaborate lighting fixtures.

The servant paused before a cherry-colored oak door. He swung the door open and inclined his head.

"I trust this room will be to your liking," he said.

Daniela entered slowly. Her eyes took in every aspect of the lavish quarters. The decor was Victorian with a rich floral bedspread, matching drapes and a small sitting area that was comprised of two Queen Anne chairs. The heavy oak furniture was even more impressive.

"It will do fine, thank you," she managed.

Emil smiled with pleasure. "Wonderful. Now, will you and Master Nicholas be staying the night?"

Her attention trailed to a portrait on the wall. It was of a beautiful dark-haired woman.

"I'm not sure. Nicholas didn't say anything about that," she told him.

Emil motioned to a door that was to the right of the room. "There is an adjoining restroom. Should you decide to stay, you will find everything you need in there. And if not, please do not hesitate to ask."

She offered him a grateful smile. "Thank you very much."

"Is there anything you require at the moment?"

"Oh, no, I'll be fine." She thought for a moment. "Wait. There is something. Would I be able to make a phone call to the U.S.A.?"

She knew that Mai must be worried. She would give her a call, if only to assure her that she was all right and making progress in finding Elaina.

Emil motioned toward a vintage telephone that sat on the table next to the bed. "Everything is at your disposal," he told her.

"Thank you," she said again.

Emil nodded and exited, closing the door softly behind him. Left alone now, Daniela began to wander about the room. She trailed careful fingers over the fine bedding and smooth furniture. She'd never quite seen a room like this before, at least not in the daylight. To think that there were people who actually lived every day of their lives like this was astounding. The closest thing she'd known to luxury was buying herself a set of gold earrings for her last birthday.

Her attention returned to the portrait on the wall. The woman was poised gracefully in an elegant evening gown, a pearl necklace complimenting her slender neck and shoulders. Her hair was piled on top of her head with a few stray curls spilling over to frame her lovely face.

Daniela looked at herself in the gilded mirror over the dresser. She pulled her hair away from her face and turned her head more to the right. For a fleeting moment, she entertained the thought of being so elegant and beautiful. The thought was short-lived. Who was she kidding? She could barely walk in heels. She didn't care about that stuff, anyway. She had more important things to think about.

Moving toward the bed, she sat carefully on the edge. She was exhausted. Her body ached, her head throbbed and she was starving. But how could she eat or sleep when her sister was missing? She had no idea if Elaina was dead or alive or suffering beneath the will of a creature like the one Nicholas had slain. Of course, denying herself food and rest wasn't helping the situation. She needed her strength if she intended to find Elaina and save her from whatever evil was holding her.

She blamed herself completely. It wasn't Nicholas's fault for taking the risks he had. It wasn't Mai's fault for not effectively covering their tracks. It was her fault. She was responsible for Elaina, and she never should've gotten herself entangled in such a situation. She should've forgotten all the people in the world who needed help and focused on the one person who needed her the most. But she'd been selfish, risking her life to fill the void that their mother had left in her heart. It was a deficit that, no matter how many mouths she fed or how many orphans she clothed, remained deep and upsetting.

A painful sob climbed its way up her throat and tears began to sting her eyes. Slowly, she fell to one side and brought her legs up onto the bed. And there, in the lonely silence amidst the wailing of her conscience, she succumbed to the twisting ache that tormented her heart.

Nicholas shot his brother an annoyed glance then stalked past him and toward the large bathroom. Undeterred, Simion pursued him. He paused in the doorway and leaned against the doorjamb.

"Come now, brother. I think I know you better than you know yourself," Simion said. "Now tell me, who is she?"

Nicholas opened a cabinet and fished through it. "I told you before, we are in a relationship."

"I would believe that, but for the fact that she is hardly your type."

He found a few first aid items. "And what is my type?"

Simion smiled. "Let's just say a bit more refined."

Nicholas hadn't really expected his brother to believe him, but he'd hoped. He and Simion shared many things and could often read the other without difficulty. But of Lord Drakon's three sons, Simion, despite his very sedate manner, was the most ruthless. Nicholas didn't need the frustration of contending with his brother's anger. However, it seemed he would have no choice. Simion could be quite relentless, and the only way to satisfy him was to tell him what he wanted to know.

Nicholas unzipped his jacket and stripped it off. "Very well, I will tell you, but you must give your word not to speak of this to anyone."

"Fine." Simion looked skeptical, but was momentarily distracted by the bloodied dressing around Nicholas's abdomen. "I see you have had an interesting night," he commented.

"Tiraghol hasn't changed since we were there last." He began unwrapping the dressing.

Simion pushed away from the door jamb. "Tiraghol? Why were you there?" he asked with concern.

"Raba witches were hired to steal the second rune. I went there to learn by whom."

His brother looked confused. "How did you know the witches were hired to steal it? When we met last you said that you'd found the tomb destroyed and the rune missing, with no trace of the thief."

With reluctance, Nicholas faced him. "The witches attacked the thief who stole the first rune, and she managed to escape with the second."

It took only a few seconds before realization seeped into Simion's eyes and his brows drew together in a frown. "Brother, please tell me that the woman you brought into this house is not the thief who stole the runes and destroyed our grandfather's tomb."

"She is."

Simion's scowl deepened. "And where is the Rune of Cythe?"

Nicholas began cleaning the dried blood from his abdomen. "It remains within her possession."

"And what, dare I ask, is the reason for that?"

"Her sister has been captured," Nicholas told him. "A man calling himself Sabbath will not release the girl until Daniela delivers the rune to him. I have reason to believe that Sabbath is one of the elders of our clan. He had to have been present the night our father revealed the location of the second rune."

His brother looked thoughtful. "How does this explain why you still haven't retrieved the Rune of Cythe from the thief?"

"She has hidden it and is not willing to release it until her sister has been found."

"She is not willing?" Again Simion barked in disbelief. "Brother, there are ways to make your adversary compliant!" With that he spun out of the room and began stalking up the hallway.

Nicholas moved quickly and slammed the door that led into the main dining room shut, blocking his brother's exit. He knew exactly where Simion was headed, and there was no way he was going to allow anyone to subject Daniela to any more abuse. Yes, she was the thief who'd stolen the runes and destroyed the tomb of his grandfather, but she'd been through enough. Her sister was lost and she'd nearly been killed the night before.

"You will leave her be," he told his brother in a very low, determined voice. "I will do this my way."

"Your way?" Simion scoffed. "You allow an enemy to keep a sacred item and you invite her into our home. How do you know that she is not still under the employ of this man who calls himself Sabbath?"

It was a good question, Nicholas decided. Yet, for reasons that eluded him, he believed Daniela had been genuine in her claim that she'd known nothing of the runes and who was after them. She'd simply taken on a job that had gone terribly wrong. And she was suffering for it.

"Allow me to worry about that. For now I need you to keep this between us. Under no circumstances is Father to learn who she really is."

Simion watched him curiously. "Why do you defend her so? Or should I even ask?"

He looked away. In truth, he had not the faintest idea why he was making such an effort to protect Daniela. It would be a simple task for his brother to force her to hand over the rune. Of this, he had no doubt. And once the stone was safely within their possession, they'd be free to seek the answers behind its missing twin. Yet, something compelled him to help Daniela. Without his assistance, her sister would more than likely be killed, and so would she.

He understood that life had been hard for her. Of course, that did nothing to justify her criminal behavior, but perhaps she deserved a reprieve.

"It is not what you think," Nicholas told his brother.

Simion folded his arms across his chest. "Then what is it?"

He sighed. "Look, I need you to trust me." He was quite ready to be done with this interrogation. "There is a matter that requires our more immediate attention." When Simion remained silent, he continued. "Last night while I was in Tiraghol, I was attacked by a shape-shifter. It was then that I discovered that I have retained the ability to morph into gargoyle form."

Surprise slowly slid over Simion's face and his arms fell away from his chest. "How is that possible? The curse was broken."

"There seems to be more than the curse at work here. If you have noticed, it is daylight and I haven't turned to stone. I am also able to control my transformation."

Nicholas brought his right hand up and flexed

it. Immediately, his nails sharpened and thick veins snaked up his arm. He gritted his teeth against the arthritic ache that assailed his joints. He relaxed it and his hand returned to normal.

Simion looked amazed. "And this was all spontaneous?"

He shook his head. "I do not think so. I believe that the transformation has been brewing for months, but only manifested last night. It took the stress of combat to produce it."

Simion leaned his back to the wall and exhaled. "So there is a chance that I too am afflicted, for I have also experienced the aches that you have."

He nodded. "The aches that we've experienced were not random, but incited by something."

"There is only one thing that can produce these outcomes," Simion said. "Sorcery."

His brother was right. Some spell had to have been cast in order for the effects of the curse to be reinitiated and altered. In this modern world, there were few who possessed the power to conjure such magic. The Raba witches had never been so skilled. But perhaps a gathering of them, coupled with the effects of the inferior spell that he and his brother had cast to ward off the ending of the curse, had made it possible. Whatever the cause, they had to discover it quickly, for there was still the chance that the curse would develop into its original state. And with the impending awakening of his uncle Gabriel, they couldn't afford the obstacle of being stone by day.

Chapter 12

The gentle rapping at the door woke Daniela from her sleep. Her eyes flew open and for a moment she thought she was still immersed in a dream. She was lying on a beautiful bed in a very lovely room. The drapes remained open, permitting the vibrant colors of the sunset in. The rapping continued and she sat up as her memory flooded back to her. She was in the home of Nicholas's family and her world had been turned upside down.

She slid from the bed and hurried to the door. She opened it and found herself face-to-face with the woman from the painting. Her hair was now a gleaming silver that had been pinned neatly into a bun, but her face looked the same.

The woman smiled at her. It was warm and genuine. "Hello, you must be Daniela."

Daniela nodded. "I am. How do you do?" she asked, feeling awkward.

She knew she looked even more of a mess after her restless sleep. The woman, who was dressed in a simple gray knee-length dress, looked radiant.

"I am well. And how are you, dear?"

She forced a smile. "I'm fine."

"Wonderful. I'm Nicholas's mother. You may call me Amelia. He certainly did not tell me how lovely you were."

Daniela blushed. "Um… Thank you."

She'd never been referred to as lovely before. In fact, she didn't think she was that good-looking, perhaps just average. She'd always envied the very fair and petite women she knew. Her dark looks weren't very appealing in her opinion.

Again Amelia smiled. "Dinner will be served in thirty minutes. Have you anything appropriate to wear?"

Daniela looked down at herself. "Um… These are my only clothes. I didn't think we would be staying here this long," she admitted.

Not that she had anything nice to wear, anyway. The few dresses she owned were cotton sundresses she reserved for Fun Days at the orphanage.

"I can remedy that. Come with me."

Daniela allowed herself to be led down the hallway to another room. It was obviously the master suite of the mansion. It was huge and sported a high domed ceiling and tall windows. A massive bed draped in a bronze canopy was the centerpiece.

Amelia led her to a large walk-in closet then disappeared inside. When she returned, she held three long evening gowns, which she placed on the bed. She took the first, a blue satin gown with a scooped neckline, and held it up against Daniela's frame.

"So tell me, how did you and Nicholas meet?" She turned Daniela to face a full-length mirror.

Daniela's heart began to race. She wasn't sure if Nicholas's mother was asking out of genuine interest, or if she suspected something was amiss and was trying to gain answers. She decided she'd better choose her story carefully, especially considering she had no idea what Nicholas had told his family already. She also wondered if this graceful and beautiful woman could possibly change into a gargoyle, as well. She decided to stick as closely to the truth as possible.

"I visited the gallery in New York," she told her. "Nicholas was kind enough to…um…assist me." She'd never been a good liar. She only hoped it wasn't obvious.

"Ah, so you've seen the gallery," Amelia said as she pulled the blue dress away and replaced it with a weightless cream number. "He and his brother have worked hard to establish themselves in your country. I am very proud of them."

Suppressing the guilt that was crawling over her, Daniela nodded. "Yes, it's a very impressive business."

Amelia removed the cream dress and brought the last one up. It was a slinky black beaded gown with a plunging back and a risqué split up one side.

"Ah, this is definitely the one. What do you think?"

"It's gorgeous," Daniela replied honestly.

The other woman slipped it off the hanger and handed it to her. "If you get changed now I can help you with your hair."

Reluctantly, Daniela accepted the dress. "Are you sure?" It was daunting just imagining the price tag. She'd be devastated if she ruined the dress.

Amelia nodded with an encouraging smile. "Of course." She took her arm and led her to an elaborate bronze and gold room divider. "You may change behind there."

"Thank you," Daniela said as she slipped behind the screen. She began peeling her clothes off and was grateful to note that the gown would adequately conceal the dressing on her thigh. On the other side of the screen she could hear Amelia moving toward the dresser and rummaging through what sounded like a box of jewelry.

"It is not often that I get to meet any of Nicholas's love interests," she commented. "You must be very special to my son."

Daniela's fingers paused on the zipper of her cargo pants. "We've been through quite a bit together."

"Well, whatever the reason, I think it is exactly what Nicholas needs. He is the wildest of my sons, and a bit of stability should do him good."

Daniela resumed changing her clothes. She didn't like the way the conversation was heading. She almost expected to hear the word *marriage* in the next few sentences. It was no surprise that Nicholas was still single. She couldn't imagine the woman who would be willing to put up with him. Not even the prospect of his wealth enticed her.

Slipping the dress over her head, she let it slide over her body. She stepped from behind the screen and looked to Amelia to gauge her opinion. Amelia turned and gasped with delight.

"Very exquisite," she remarked as she pulled Daniela to face the mirror again. "I am sure Nicholas will be very pleased."

Daniela gawked at her reflection. The dress was perfect. It clung to her body as if made for her and showed off her attributes quite nicely.

"Wow," she said, a soft smile on her lips. She'd never worn anything so nice before.

"Hold your hair up, dear," Amelia instructed.

Daniela complied and watched as Amelia placed a silver necklace about her neck. Weighed by what appeared to be a small teardrop pearl, it dangled just above her cleavage.

Amelia's eyes flashed with approval in the mirror. "And this is for you. It's always been one of my favorite pieces."

Slowly, Daniela's hand moved to caress the delicate bit of jewelry. "Oh, I couldn't," she protested softly.

It was bad enough that she and Nicholas were deceiving his family. She didn't feel right about taking jewelry from his mother. It was odd— had she been hired to steal the item it wouldn't have been a problem. There was just something about Amelia that made her warm inside. She seemed very sweet and motherly, very nurturing.

Amelia turned Daniela to face her. "Think of it as a gift. It has been a long wait for the woman who can tame my son, and you seem to be off to a wonderful start."

She found herself being ushered over to a vanity and into a chair.

"And now, let us do something with your hair." Amelia pulled a silver brush and comb out of the drawer. "Would you prefer your hair up or down and framing your face?"

"Up, I think," Daniela responded. She wondered if it was obvious that she wasn't accustomed to discussing hairstyles.

Amelia began running the comb through Daniela's hair. A sharp pain shot through the back of her scalp and she winced. Immediately, Amelia stopped combing.

"What is it?"

Daniela brought a hand to the back of her head and touched the sore spot. It was the place she'd been struck by the shape-shifter in Tiraghol. When she removed her hand, her fingertips were smeared with a small amount of blood.

"You're hurt!" Amelia gently parted Daniela's hair to examine the injury.

"It's nothing." Daniela tried to appear aloof. "I fell while I was hiking."

She couldn't tell if Amelia believed her or not,

but the other woman fixed her with a scrutinizing stare in the mirror.

"Did you seek medical attention?"

"No," Daniela replied. "I didn't think it was necessary. It's not bothering me."

The older woman stared at her for a few more seconds before speaking. "I see. Well, I will tend to it for you."

She crossed the bedroom and slipped into another room. Daniela released a breath that she hadn't been aware she was holding. She found her reflection in the mirror. She wanted nothing more than to leave. She didn't belong there and didn't want to be there. But she had to be patient, she told herself. She had to play Nicholas's game. And once she found her sister, she'd be able to leave Romania and all the insanity it entailed for good.

Nicholas waited for his father's response after having relayed his experience in Tiraghol, omitting any mention of Daniela, of course. Lord

Victor sat at the head of the main dining-hall table, gazing into the flickering fires of the heavy cast-iron candelabra centerpiece.

"And you say you've recovered the Rune of Cythe?" Lord Victor asked.

"Yes. I managed to track the thief who took it from the cemetery. Retrieving it was a simple task after that."

Nicholas looked to his brother, who was seated at their father's right. Simion was still quite un-happy with the situation involving Daniela, but he remained silent.

Lord Victor nodded in approval. "And where is the rune now?"

Again Nicholas exchanged looks with Simion. "I have secured it. As we are still unsure of how information is being passed, I would prefer to keep the new location exclusively to myself."

Their father was silent for a moment. His eyes were narrowed as he considered what Nicholas proposed. "Very well," he agreed at last. "As long as the rune remains secure. Now, about your transformation, I can only speculate that the one called Sabbath has been attempting to awaken Gabriel without the use of the runes. If he has hired Raba witches to perform the sorcery, their craft was more than likely incapable of dissolving the spell Agatha set nearly three hundred years ago."

Simion nodded in agreement. "And once that had failed, he resorted to stealing the runes."

"Precisely," Lord Victor agreed. "Only the sorcery had not dissipated without effect. Somehow it managed to mend the spell you and your brother had attempted to cast during the night the curse was broken. And the end result is what Nicholas experienced."

Nicholas reclined in his chair. It was a perfectly plausible explanation. There weren't many witches left who possessed the powers of their ancestors. Any inferior sorcery would serve only to disrupt the course of an ancient spell, but never eliminate it. They'd more than discovered this during their quest to break the gargoyle curse. It was this that caused Nicholas the most worry.

"The prospect of having this ability at my will would almost seem a blessing, for I have missed the strength and speed we'd enjoyed," he admitted. "But there is no certainty that it ends here. The spell may progress to what it once was."

The mere thought of having to surrender humanity and be drawn back into the vicious cycle of being stone by day and gargoyle by night was agonizing.

Their father nodded. "For this reason we cannot afford to wait. Your mother and I have located Agatha's successor. She has lived all these years in a village called Sussex."

Hope flickered in Simion's eyes. "And do you think she has the answers we seek?"

"It is a possibility. Many years ago she was Agatha's pupil. I would imagine that she would know more about the runes and their powers than anyone else. Sorcery can always be altered, and she may have a way for us to deactivate the runes."

The large double doors opened and their cousin Andrew entered. Lord Victor waved to him.

"Ah, Andrew, nice of you to join us. I was hoping to have an audience with you before you returned to the United States."

Andrew approached and exchanged greetings with everyone present. "My flight leaves in the morning. I thought I should stop over and give you an update."

Lord Victor leaned forward, clasping his hands on the table in front of him. "And have you learned anything of significance?"

"Actually, I have. The man I have following Stefan has reported to me that he has been frequenting witch hovels and apothecaries."

"Are any of them connected to the Raba witch clan?" Lord Victor asked with peaking interest.

Discomfort crossed Andrew's face. "I'm not sure. Nothing was specified."

Lord Victor sighed. "Andrew, you must be more astute. We are gathering evidence here."

"I apologize," Andrew said. "I didn't think it was necessary. Stefan's actions clearly implicate him in the crimes that have been committed."

"That may be so, but every bit of detail is essential at this point."

Andrew inclined his head. "I will have this information to you by tomorrow."

Lord Victor took a sip of wine and nodded. "If Stefan has engaged in these activities, I will see to it that he is summoned before the Darcian Council."

Nicholas was in agreement. The Darcian Council was the highest body among the Drakon and Ananovian witch clans. Originally formed when an alliance had been created between the two clans, the Council had been in practice for centuries and comprised fifteen members of both clans, his father being one of them. Its purpose was to retain a balance to the magnitude of sorcery used. Spells of great proportion weren't to be cast or commissioned without first being approved. If the laws were broken, one could very well be forced into exile. It had been many years since the council had been drawn together, as much had changed after the wars with other witch clans had ended.

Andrew took a seat. "Has there been any news of the Rune of Cythe?"

Nicholas chose to respond. "It has been retrieved." This was all he offered.

Andrew had been a longstanding friend, and he'd proven himself to be both loyal and dedicated to their clan, but at this point Nicholas wasn't willing to put anyone above suspicion.

Andrew looked relieved. "Excellent! And have we any knowledge of where the Rune of Moloch may be?"

"Nothing substantial…" Nicholas began, but his voice trailed off as the dining-room door opened.

Nicholas's mother, Lady Amelia, entered, and she wasn't alone. Andrew's teenage daughter,

Elsthbeth, and Daniela were with her. Daniela however, looked nothing like the woman who'd caused him so much grief over the past few days. Standing before him was a tall and incredibly beautiful vixen. Gone were her unflattering cargo pants and pullover. Instead, she wore a very elegant black dress that hugged her luscious form. Ample breasts strained against the plunging neckline, and a long and shapely leg peeked through a very scandalous split.

Lord Victor and Simion stood as was custom in their family whenever a woman entered the room. Nicholas managed to regain enough composure to ease himself out of his chair.

Elthsbeth came to him immediately and looped an arm into his. "Is she your girlfriend?" she whispered near his ear.

Nicholas was able to drag his eyes away from Daniela to find Elsthbeth looking up at him with a mixture of jealousy and humor. He mustered a smile, but said nothing.

Lord Victor extended his hands in welcome to

Daniela. "Ah, so this is the lovely lady Nicholas has been hiding."

Daniela placed slender hands into his and was drawn into a warm embrace. Nicholas couldn't stop his gaze from trailing along the smooth curve of her shoulders and down her back.

She was passed to Andrew who bowed graciously and placed a kiss on her hand. "Lovely indeed," he said with a smile.

Simion offered her a similar gesture, but with a depreciation of zeal. After Daniela had exchanged greetings with everyone, Lady Amelia guided her to the chair beside Nicholas.

For a brief moment his eyes locked with Daniela's and the emotion he read there was something he'd not seen before. There was a certain softness about her, a vulnerability. He knew her present situation was far from comfortable, but it couldn't have been avoided. He needed to consult his family on what had taken place, and there was no way he was going to let her out of his sight—at least not as long as she had the rune.

All discussion of the stones, witches and curses ceased at that point. His mother took it upon herself to delve deeper into his relationship with Daniela, and his father joined her. Simion remained silent, but hid his discontent well.

To Nicholas's surprise, Daniela responded to their questions with ease and confidence. As the dinner progressed, he found it difficult to focus on the conversations that passed among them. He couldn't keep his eyes off the woman at his side. Beneath the flickering candlelight, she looked radiant. He noted the way her ripe lips would curve ever so slightly in a modest smile whenever a joke was told. And the way she inclined her head to one side when listening; it was an action that often sent a wayward curl of ebony silk trickling over her cleavage.

Although she masked it well, he knew that his undivided attention was adding to her displeasure, but his behavior was completely justifiable. They were pretending to be lovers. Surely it would be odd if he didn't demonstrate his affection for her. With this obligation in mind, he extended an arm over the back of her chair, draping her in his warmth. His fingers found a soft spot on her arm and there they traced a pattern in lazy distraction.

Her entire body tensed beneath his caress and she paused midsentence. Nicholas offered her a smile. She recovered quickly, finishing her sentence. He could tell that she didn't appreciate his attention. He'd certainly never had that problem before. It was not unusual to have women groveling for a night in his bed. Then again, Daniela was unique in most ways.

The soft scraping of chairs on the floor drew him out of his thoughts. It seemed the meal had ended. He had to look at his plate to determine what they'd eaten. He stood and pulled out Daniela's chair for her. Everyone said their good-nights. Lord Victor, Simion and Andrew headed to the sitting room, while Elsthbeth excused herself to her bedchamber.

Daniela exchanged kisses with Lady Amelia then turned to Nicholas. She stepped close and a flicker of dread registered in her eyes. Nicholas watched her for a few seconds, oddly anticipating the taste of her on his lips again.

He reached out and placed a gentle hand on her waist before pulling her close. His head dipped and their lips brushed. The kiss was fleeting, but it awoke every nerve in his body. He quickly set her aside and turned away. He didn't appreciate the desire she was evoking in him. It was only due to the fact that he'd gone so long without a woman, he told himself. His brother was quite right, he did prefer his women far more refined. Daniela was hardly his type.

"Good night," she said quietly.

He responded and listened to her slip from the room. Once the door was shut, he headed toward the sitting room where his father and brother had resigned.

"Nicholas." His mother's voice stopped him. "May I have a word with you?"

He sighed. He knew that tone and braced himself for the worst. Slowly, he turned to face her. "Yes?"

She was standing behind her chair with her hands braced on its elaborate frame. The look she gave him was contemplative. "Daniela is a lovely girl," she commented. "Are you happy with her?"

He sighed, wondering where the conversation was heading. "I am." He offered nothing more.

Lady Amelia sauntered toward a mirror that stood over the lacquered buffet table. "And what of Daniela, is she happy?" She adjusted her hair.

"Yes, mother. Why do you ask? Has she said something to you?"

"One does not need words to relay sadness, my son." She looked at him then. "I can read it in her eyes."

"Perhaps you have discerned incorrectly. I know nothing of what you speak."

She turned to face him. "No? Then what do you know of the injury at the back of her head? Or better yet, explain why she flinches at your touch."

His eyes narrowed on her. "Surely you do not think I've done something to the girl. I would never harm a woman, you know this."

"I am not accusing you, my son. I have not raised you to be abusive," she said. "I only wish to know what you conceal from your family. Something tells me that Daniela is more than you say."

His mother had always been overly perceptive, and as he'd feared, she'd somehow suspected the deception. Nevertheless, he'd already decided to withhold any information. He'd taken a risk by revealing Daniela's true identity to his brother. And he'd only done so because he had complete faith in the bond between them. For centuries they'd fought together, blindly trusting each other with their lives. Simion understood him and would do what it took to defend him.

Nicholas had enough to contend with at the moment. With the Rune of Moloch still missing and the possible resurrection of the curse, he certainly didn't need the added distraction of thinking about Daniela. She was a momentary hindrance that he would gladly be done with as soon as they located her sister and the Rune of Cythe was returned to the Drakon clan.

He turned away. "Leave it be, Mother," he told her. "I will reveal everything to you when the time comes. But I am sorry. Now is not that time."

That said, he stalked toward the sitting room.

Chapter 13

Daniela tossed beneath the bedspread for what seemed the hundredth time. She couldn't sleep. After her nap earlier in the day, she was barely tired and she couldn't stop thinking about Elaina. She'd managed to contact Mai and give her an update on what was happening. Mai hadn't gone to the police to report Elaina's kidnapping because she'd been warned that Elaina would be killed upon the first suspicion of police involvement. They'd also not received information about the drop-off point for the rune yet.

Daniela looked at the clock: 12:37 a.m. Morning

couldn't come fast enough for her. She was ready to go back out there and follow whatever leads Nicholas had come up with. Her heart ached at the thought of her baby sister all alone for so long. She was desperate and she needed answers. And she felt she was wasting precious time.

She groaned and turned again. This time she sat up and turned on the bedside lamp. Soft light filled the room and her gaze wandered over to the window. The drapes had been drawn, but she recalled how wide it was. She was sorely tempted to get dressed and slip out into the early morning. But where would she go? She didn't even know what Nicholas's next plan of action was.

She slumped against the fat pillows on the bed and sighed. The wisest thing to do was be patient. She was reaching to turn off the lamp when the door opened and Nicholas walked in. With a gasp, she gripped the bedspread and drew it up to her shoulders, concealing the thin nightgown that his mother had given her to wear.

Nicholas spared her a glance. "You are still awake," he commented as he closed the door behind him.

She blinked at him as he began to unbutton the crisp white shirt he wore. "What are you doing?" she asked.

"Go to sleep. It is late." He slipped the garment off and it fell haphazardly to the floor.

Daniela pulled the bedspread higher as he approached the other side of the bed. "You're not planning to sleep in here, are you?" she asked with no effort to mask her disapproval.

He sat on the edge of the bed and slipped a shoe off. "In case you have forgotten, we are here under the pretense of being in a relationship. It would be unusual for us to sleep in separate quarters."

Daniela scowled at his broad back. She refused to believe that he couldn't find another place to sleep without his family knowing.

"Unusual or not, I'm not sharing a bed with

you," she protested. "This house is large enough. I'm sure I can find somewhere else to sleep."

She tossed the bedding aside and swung her legs down. Before her toes touched the soft carpet, Nicholas reached out and took hold of one of her wrists.

"You will do no such thing," he said very quietly.

She glared at him. She'd never shared a bed with a man before, let alone a tall and beautiful male with rippling muscles and too much sex appeal. The bed wasn't exactly accommodating either. It was a standard queen-size, which wouldn't leave very much space between them.

"I'm not sleeping in this bed with you, Nicholas," she said with as much determination as she could muster.

He watched her for a few seconds then his hold relented. "Do as you wish," he told her. "But I will have you know that I was forced to reveal your identity to my brother. He would be pleased to find you wandering about this house in the middle of the night. I am sure you two will have a lot to discuss."

About to get out of the bed, Daniela froze. She'd been wondering if Nicholas had told his brother who she really was. At dinner Simion hadn't said one word to her and the occasional looks he'd cast her way hadn't been very friendly, either. Now she understood why. And if Simion was anything like his brother, he was the last person she wanted to run into down a dark hallway.

There seemed to be no alternative. It was only one night, she told herself. And it was already almost morning. All she had to do was stay awake and get up as soon as it was light. Nicholas seemed tired, too. If she was lucky, he would simply pass out and sleep until the sun rose.

She eased back beneath the covers and pulled them up to her chin. She suddenly remembered that all she wore was the light garment and that only reached her at midthigh. At the moment it was bunched up around her waist and to make matters worse, she wasn't wearing any panties.

Behind her she could hear Nicholas stripping away his remaining attire. The soft *clank* of his belt falling to the floor was followed by the sweeping sound of his pants being removed. She hoped he didn't sleep naked. In slow degrees she inched herself to the very edge of the bed. She could hear him laughing, the sound deep and sensuous.

"What's so funny?" she asked.

"Your antics," was all he supplied.

A draft scooted in under the covers as he peeled them away. The bed creaked softly beneath his weight and immediately the heat of his body wrapped about her legs. Daniela tensed, trying to gauge the distance between them. The bed suddenly seemed a few inches smaller. That or she'd underestimated how large the man was. She had a clear view of the floor. If she moved any closer to the edge she would find herself on it. For a moment, she entertained the thought of doing just that—sleeping on the floor. It was quickly dashed, for her body still ached. Exacerbating that could hardly be beneficial, especially at a time like this when her health and strength would be necessary to face whatever evil she had to in order to save Elaina.

The bed creaked again and she felt Nicholas moving toward her. She turned quickly to face him, wondering what he was about. He was reaching for the lamp, but paused. He looked at her, his eyes fleeting over her face.

"You have been crying," he said.

She wanted to look away, but couldn't. She was held fast by his attention. It seemed gentle, and if she didn't know any better, she would actually think he cared.

"No," she replied softly.

A smile tugged at one corner of his firm lips. "And who said a good thief made a good liar?" When she remained silent he continued. "My mother told me that you have suffered an injury to your head."

"It's nothing. She took care of it."

"And what of the bullet wound to your thigh?"

Again she wondered why he seemed so concerned. There was hardly the need to feign interest, not now when there was no one about. Nevertheless, she swallowed her inquiry. She'd made a promise to be more civil with him, and now seemed as good a time as ever to start.

"It only hurts a little," she admitted truthfully. "I've changed the dressing a few times, too. I'll be okay."

His attention drifted to the necklace that Amelia had given her. "It was a gift from your mother." She didn't want him to think she'd stolen it.

He acknowledged what she'd said with a grunt and his eyes remained on her. She found that she still couldn't look away from him. He was so handsome beneath the soft glow of the lamp with his wild hair falling freely about his face and shoulders.

Flinching uncomfortably, she tried to disrupt

the intimacy of the situation. "Did you have a chance to talk to your family about what you learned last night?"

"I did."

"And what did they say? Is there any news about the man who's holding my sister?"

He sighed. "We have reason to believe that he is one of the elders of our family. His activities of late have been questionable. Tomorrow he will be summoned before our clan's council and expected to provide an explanation for his actions."

"Will you be there?" she asked.

"No. My brother and I have other business to attend to," he replied. "We are going to seek the advice of a sorceress. We only hope that she has some insight on how to neutralize the runes."

"Neutralize the runes?" Daniela quickly pushed herself up on her elbows. "You can't do that, not now."

She frowned up at him. It seemed he was doing everything but trying to help her find her sister. Elaina was still out there, and the longer they took the more she would suffer.

"There is no choice," Nicholas told her. "We will have to take the chance if it becomes available."

She shook her head in disbelief. "And what do you think will happen to my sister if her captors learn that those runes are useless? Do you think they will simply let her go?"

Tears began to blur her vision and she suddenly felt very much alone. If he wasn't going to make a determined effort to help her then she was wasting her time there. Beneath the covers she quickly adjusted her nightgown then tossed the bedspread off.

"I see I have to take control of this situation. I'm not going to sit and wait just to learn my sister is dead."

She tried to swing her legs out of the bed, but Nicholas placed a muscled arm about her waist and held her where she was.

"And just what do you intend to do?" he asked.

She fought to pry his arm away. "Let me go! I'm going to find my sister." Tears slipped down her temples and she stifled a sob. "I'll go back to the monastery if I have to. I'll make them tell me where she is."

She'd always protected her sister. Even when they were in Brazil and their father's anger and alcoholism had erupted into a fierce tirade of abuse. She'd never forgive herself if something happened to Elaina. She wouldn't know how to go on living.

Nicholas gripped her flailing arms and brought them over her head, pinning her to mattress. "The only thing you are going to do is get yourself killed."

She heaved beneath him, eager to get away. "Just leave me alone, please." Her tears were flowing freely now. "She's just a kid. She shouldn't be out there. It's my fault!"

"Stop this." He said firmly. "To act without thinking will do none of us any good. You must be patient."

Fighting him was useless. Her strength was nothing compared to his. Her movements stilled and she turned her face away. She didn't want him to see her cry, but the weight of every-thing—of her entire life—came rushing over her. It wasn't fair that their mother had left them. Or that she'd had no choice but to steal to survive.

"You are not alone in this, Daniela," Nicholas said in a voice that was surprisingly very gen-tle. "I made an agreement with you and I will see it to its end. But you will have to trust me."

The ache in her heart was overwhelming. She could feel Nicholas's arms moving about her and soon found herself encased within his warm embrace.

He held her close to him, his fingers carefully stroking her hair. "I will do whatever I can to find your sister, I promise you."

Despite herself, she clung to him. There was a certain security in his arms she'd never ex-perienced before. She felt safe and protected.

And as she listened to his words of promise, she believed him. If anyone could help her find Elaina, it was Nicholas.

"We have to do something, Nicholas. Time is running out...." she started to say.

He pulled away from her and looked into her eyes. "I need you to trust me and to be patient."

She wanted so much to share his confidence. Perhaps he knew something that she didn't, or in his many years of life had encountered a similar situation. He was right and she knew it. She needed to stay calm and she needed to exert a little patience.

She nodded. "I'll try."

His gaze softened and he continued to hold her at arm's length. Her body yearned to return to his embrace, and before she could stop herself, she looped her arms about his neck and closed the distance between them. She'd never needed anyone before, but right now she needed his warmth, his comfort, his protection. She needed him.

Her gesture was unexpected and she felt his body tense. It lasted only a fleeting moment before his arms wound about her again. Strong fingers traced a gentle path along her spine and she shivered. After a few moments Nicholas lowered her head to the pillow.

"It is late. You should sleep," he said.

She nodded slowly, then Nicholas reached out and brushed a tear from her cheek. A stray curl had settled there too and he tucked it behind her ear. She allowed him to finish his task without objection. There was a tenderness about him that she would've never expected. It was difficult to believe that beneath his very hard exterior was this gentler side.

He didn't move. He just watched her and his attention raked the length of her body. Her heart began to beat even harder, and Daniela suddenly realized that she was no longer beneath the covers, but stretched out before him in nothing but the sheer nightgown. The cool air tautened her nipples and they rose beneath the gossamer fabric, summoning his attention.

When he met her gaze again, his eyes blazed with an emerald fire. They penetrated her, scorching her insides and making her acutely aware of her nakedness beneath the flimsy garment. Her skin began to prickle and she swallowed.

Slowly, Nicholas's head dipped and without taking his eyes from her, he tasted her lips. The kiss was brief, but a sensuous invitation that sent her heart into a new chaotic riot. He withdrew slightly. The intensity of his stare couldn't be misread—he wanted her. Yet he waited. It was as if he was giving her an opportunity to protest.

Daniela remained silent, but her mind screamed a warning that she was nothing to him. He was centuries old, otherworldly...a gargoyle. Yet at that moment none of it mattered. She couldn't deny her intense attraction for him. Her body yearned for his touch and ached for his kisses. Perhaps it was out of vulnerability that she felt this way, but she didn't care. If nothing else, she would have her memories when it was all over and they went their separate ways.

When she made no objection, Nicholas's mouth found hers a second time. His kiss was very patient and tender. He coaxed her lips apart and his tongue slid into her mouth. A warm sensation began building inside her. It started within the pit of her belly and trickled down to pool in the soft place between her thighs.

As before, he withdrew from her and their eyes met. He hid nothing. His intent was clear: he was going to possess her. One large hand came up and he slipped the weightless strap of the nightgown from her shoulder, dragging it low on her arm so that her breast was revealed.

His hand moved to cover the soft mound, gently kneading her erect nipple. Daniela's cheeks flushed and she fought to calm her breathing. Nicholas's hand slid beneath the fabric to claim her other breast, which was pleading for his attention. "Have you ever been touched by a man?" he asked in a heavy voice.

His question was unexpected and she blinked at him. So scattered were her thoughts that it took a few seconds for her to decipher his meaning. She shook her head, suddenly feeling quite embarrassed. Being a virgin at her age was almost unheard of.

He didn't look surprised. Instead, he dragged the other strap of her nightgown down, completely exposing her chest. He paused briefly to gaze upon her, then, with a feral growl, he claimed her right breast. His mouth, hot and wet, enclosed over her erect nipple and he devoured it greedily.

Daniela gasped, her back arching off the bed. She'd never experienced anything quite so wonderful. She could feel his thick, hard shaft pressing against her thigh beneath the bedspread. The knowledge that she had the ability to arouse him emboldened her and she brought timid fingers up along the sleek muscles of his arm.

He seemed to revel in her touch and the intensity of his mouth increased. He moved to worship her other breast while his hand found its way beneath the skirt of her nightgown. Roughened fingers caressed the sensitive skin there, moving lower until they lingered just above her soft mound of flesh.

His mouth found her lips again, smothering the gasp she emitted as two lean fingers found their way into the folds of her womanhood. Her legs began to tremble and fell slightly apart, encouraging his exploration. She was well lubricated and his fingers slipped easily over her sensitive little bud that was at present throbbing with an ache she'd never experienced before.

Nicholas groaned into her mouth, filling her chest with a deep and savage sound. Her hands continued to move over him and she enjoyed the feel of his powerful muscles flexing beneath her touch.

The probing of his fingers continued. They circled the moist entrance of her tight passage, taunting her into madness. Years of suppressed sexual frustration seemed to cascade over her and with a soft cry, she spread her thighs a little wider. As if by their own accord, her hips began to undulate in a slow and very shameless rhythm. She wanted him—needed to feel him inside her.

When she thought she could bear his teasing no longer, one lean finger eased into her. Her body clenched about the invading member and she arched higher off the bed. Nicholas's finger moved deeper inside her, slipping higher until the roughened skin of his palm could be felt against her delicate flesh. She ground herself against his palm as she was overtaken by a yearning to be filled by him.

His firm lips traced a path from her mouth to her neck and it was there that he engaged his next onslaught. It was becoming increasingly difficult for Daniela to breathe. Her breath was coming in short gasps and her nipples grazed his skin with each intake.

To her dismay, she felt his finger leaving her body. He lifted his head then and their eyes met. The desire she read on his face was daunting. His hand came up and she could see that his fingers were slick with moisture. Slowly, deliberately and without severing their stare, Nicholas slipped his fingers into his mouth.

In awe, Daniela watched as he licked them clean. A bolt of something hot shot through her and a fire erupted between her thighs. There was something decidedly primal about Nicholas that called to her. It made her want to spread her thighs and surrender herself to whatever perversions he was inclined to.

He sat up and slipped the rumpled nightgown from her trembling body. He gazed upon her nakedness for a few seconds before kneeling and stripping his own tight-fitting boxers off.

Daniela swallowed as she trailed a path down his nakedness. The man was incredibly beautiful. He remained kneeled above her with his muscled body gleaming in the lamplight. His abdomen, as she'd recalled, was hard and perfect. His thighs were sculpted and exuded power. And to complete the package, he sported a large, thick erection. She used every bit of her will to avoid looking at it, but it was hardly a thing to be ignored. The sheer anticipation of having him sink it into her was sending her thoughts into a dizzying spin.

Nicholas spread her thighs and moved to kneel between them. He drew the bedspread over them and his massive body descended over her. She emitted another little cry as his mouth found her breasts again. His sensuous administrations seared a path down her abdomen and his head disappeared beneath the bedspread. Nicholas gripped her behind her knees and raised her thighs as high as her body would permit.

What came next was completely unexpected

and her body was racked by a pulsating shudder. Nicholas's head moved between her thighs and she could feel his hot mouth enclose over her. Like a man starved, he feasted, sucking and licking—extracting a wanton moan from her. Her fingers wove into his hair and held him in place. It wasn't long before she was engaged within the throes of an intense orgasm. Spasms rippled through her body and she cried out.

Only then did Nicholas resurface. His eyes were dark with a burning and hungry lust. Almost bereft of her strength, Daniela looked up at him through the mist in her eyes. There was definitely no turning back now. She braced herself for what was to come. Her virginity was about to be lost and to an ageless gargoyle. Strangely, it felt completely right.

Nicholas positioned himself above her and leaned in for a kiss. She could taste herself on his lips and she returned his kiss with the passion of a woman who was ready to be possessed.

The tip of his manhood nudged at her opening, gently probing until she moaned.

"Please…" she gasped before she could stop herself. "I need you."

That seemed to be all the encouragement he needed. With a feral growl, he pressed into her. Daniela's body tensed as a sharp pain erupted in that spot where their bodies were joined. Nicholas pulled her into his arms and placed a soft kiss against her cheek.

"The pain will be over soon," he told her.

She held on to him and they lay like that for what seemed an eternity. The patience Nicholas exerted astounded her. She would have never guessed he possessed such traits. And as he'd promised, it wasn't long before she acclimated to the new sensation of being filled by him.

He must've sensed the tension being released from her body for he started to move within her. The pressure of his gentle thrusting fueled the fire building within her. She drew in a breath, wanting him deeper. His pace quickened and her body rose to meet each thrust. Together they climaxed, and as he poured his hot seed into her, his name trickled out on her breath.

Chapter 14

Nicholas entered the bedroom quietly. He moved to stand over the bed and his eyes raked over the slender form beneath the bedspread. The night he'd spent with Daniela had been unlike any encounter he'd had with any woman. Possessing her beautiful body had gone beyond the physical. The feelings she'd left him with were more than disturbing. It seemed they shared an emotional connection, and there was something that compelled him to protect her.

She'd shown him a vulnerable part of herself, one she hid very well beneath her independence and determination. Although he did admire those qualities, it had been intriguing to have a glimpse of the softer Daniela…almost too intriguing. After their lovemaking, they'd lain there in the darkness and talked. She'd told him about her life and the hardships she'd endured. And in return, he'd talked about his struggles and his experiences as a gargoyle. He'd also told her the truth about the rune stones and the twelve statues.

He slipped his leather jacket on. Sleep had evaded him and he'd spent the past hour lying beside her with random thoughts plaguing his mind. It had saddened his heart to see her cry. She was ready to risk her life once again to save her little sister, which was completely understandable. Her sister was really the only person she had in the world.

Driven by her despair, he'd decided that waiting was no longer an option. Even if Stefan was brought to trial, such an investigation could take weeks, especially with no solid evidence. Every moment wasted brought Daniela's sister closer to a sure death. If Stefan was indeed Sabbath, then Nicholas was going to find out before the sun rose. As Simion had said, there were many ways to make one's adversary compliant. He reached beneath the lamp and flicked the switch off, then turned and headed for the door.

Stefan Drakon resided in an ill-kept estate set back into the trees, away from civilization. It had taken Nicholas nearly forty-five minutes to locate it. Stefan lived alone as was his preference. An eccentric recluse, he preferred the company of darkness and silence to that of his family. Nicholas knew very little about him— his habits, his personality and even his reason for being the way he was. However, until now Stefan had never been a cause for concern.

Nicholas climbed the chipped steps that led up to the porch of the Victorian-style house. The wood creaked under his weight and his shadow swayed beneath the light of a lantern that had been strung to the roof. A mild breeze gathered up the dried leaves that were strewn about, haphazardly rearranging them from corner to corner.

Gripping the rusty door knocker, Nicholas attempted a knock, but the thing came off in his hand. He placed it on the rail of the porch, and before he could do anything else, the door creaked open. Stefan stood in the portal, glaring at him.

"What are you doing here at this hour?" was the only greeting he offered.

"May I come in?" Nicholas asked. "I wish to have a few words with you."

A look of suspicion crossed Stefan's face. "Concerning what?"

"The runes." Nicholas watched him closely for any indication of discomfort.

Stefan provided none. Instead, he seemed to take a moment to consider his request then he stepped aside. Nicholas entered and was led down a wide hallway. His eyes missed nothing as they took in the passage and the rooms that branched off from it. He was looking for any clues that would indicate that Stefan was indeed dabbling in sorcery.

The sitting room they entered was no different from the rest of the house. The rugs were worn, furniture was old and every surface was covered with dust or a mound of books.

Stefan motioned to a faded King Louis chair. "Have a seat." He sat in a large leather armchair. "Now, what is this about?"

Nicholas reclined in the chair, placing an ankle on a knee. "It was reported that you have been paying frequent visits to witch hovels," he said bluntly.

He hadn't come there under false pretenses. He needed answers and he was prepared to do whatever it took to acquire them.

Stefan leaned forward, pinning him with a dark stare. "And what has my personal business to do with you, or anyone else for that matter?"

"In light of the situation at hand, I am forced to wonder if it is simply a mere coincidence."

"Ahh," Stefan nodded. "I see what this is about. You have come here to accuse me of stealing the runes."

Nicholas continued to watch him. "Can you blame me for my suspicion? Since the night of the gathering of elders, your words and actions have implicated you."

"I have done nothing to deviate from the laws of our clan." He stood and focused his attention on a threadbare medieval tapestry that embellished the wall. "Therefore, I need not explain myself to anyone."

"I'm not sure the Darcian Council will agree." Nicholas sat forward. "If there is something you must reveal I suggest you do it now while my offer is extended in good graces."

Stefan turned slowly to face him and the look on his face was far from appreciative. "Do not threaten, boy! I suggest you leave my home before things become a bit unpleasant for you."

Standing, Nicholas crossed his arms over his chest. He wasn't going to be so easily deterred.

"I am not leaving until you provide me with a legitimate explanation. I want to know who the witches were that you felt compelled to see and why."

"Oh, you will be leaving," Stefan said as he advanced toward him. "And you will do so now!"

He lunged at Nicholas, gripping him by the collar of his jacket and slamming him into a bookcase. Books clamored to the floor as the shelf toppled over. Nicholas gripped Stefan's hands and pried them from his clothing. He was amazed by the strength the other man exerted. Even with Nicholas's gargoyle abilities playing a role, Stefan was a difficult opponent.

Still holding on to him, Nicholas propelled the other man across the room and Stefan went down on a coffee table, which crumbled beneath his weight.

Nicholas frowned at him. Stefan's reaction was certainly unexpected. It increased Nicholas's suspicions—perhaps he *was* Sabbath.

There was no logical reason why he would re-fuse to provide an explanation for his actions, especially if there was a chance that he would face trial for treason.

Stefan wasted no time in getting to his feet. He snatched up one of the table legs and swung it at Nicholas, who caught his arm. A struggle followed and Nicholas managed to pin the other man to the wall.

"Are you the one they call Sabbath?" Nicholas demanded. "Where is the child?"

His teeth barred, Stefan struggled wildly. "I know nothing of what you speak! Perhaps it is you who has brought this upon us!"

His struggling continued and with a sud-den burst of strength, he thrust Nicholas off. Nicholas stumbled into a vintage floor lamp, knocking it to the ground. The shade smashed and the bulb flickered out. The room was sud-denly bathed in darkness but he could clearly see Stefan hunched over on the floor a few feet away. His moans were agonizing and to

Nicholas's disbelief two massive shadows sprang from the other man's back. Stefan grabbed his head just as two horns jarred out of his skull. He'd transformed into a gargoyle.

Daniela awoke with a very warm feeling inside which vanished immediately when she realized what had taken place the night before. She sat up in bed and squinted against the pale sunlight that peeked in through the drapes. Glancing about the room she realized Nicholas was gone. The scent of him lingered on her skin, filling her senses and summoning memories of the night's passion. Nicholas had surprised her. He'd been a gentle and patient lover, and the pleasure he'd incited had been unimaginable. Yet, she regretted the encounter for it had revealed emotions within her that she didn't want or need.

Despite the closeness she'd experienced last night, now she felt only shame. She was certain she was just another notch on Nicholas's belt.

He hadn't even bothered to stay the remainder of the night with her.

She, on the other hand, had come to realize that it had been more than an irresistible attraction that had lured her to him. She'd begun to fall in love with Nicholas Drakon.

This surprised her for he was hardly the type of man she'd fantasized about. She'd envisioned herself with a soft-spoken, patient and understanding gentleman—the complete opposite of her father. Yet Nicholas, while nothing like her father, was also a far cry from her Prince Charming. Nevertheless, there was just something about the strength and authority he possessed that brought her blood to a rapid boil.

She swung her legs out of the bed. She'd made a big mistake, but she couldn't waste time dwelling on it. Elaina needed her. Nicholas had made a promise to her last night. He'd said that he was willing to do whatever it took to help her find her sister. She only hoped that he kept his word.

She hurried to the wardrobe and retrieved her

clothing, which to her surprise had been laundered. Nicholas had said that today he and his brother would be paying a visit to a witch. She had every intention of going with them.

After a quick shower, she hurried down the stairs and encountered the servant Nicholas had referred to as Emil.

"Good morning," she said in greeting.

He welcomed her with a smile. "Good morning, my lady. Did you have a pleasant night?"

She looked down, suddenly feeling quite embarrassed. "I did, thank you."

"Wonderful, and will you be wanting some breakfast?"

"Oh, no," she declined. "But thank you. Is Nicholas still here?"

Emil pointed down a hallway. "Follow the hall to the garage. I last saw him there."

She nodded with a smile and headed down the passage. She paused before the door and took a deep breath. She wasn't sure how to behave with Nicholas after the night they'd shared. Of course, she had no expectations of him. It was what it was—a night of passion and nothing more. That however, did nothing to decrease her discomfort.

Inhaling again, she turned the door handle and entered a moderately sized garage. She saw Nicholas immediately. He stood behind an SUV and looked as if he was packing things into it.

She stopped within a few feet of him. "Good morning." She looked everywhere but at him.

He acknowledged her greeting with a grunt. Daniela fought the discomfort rising within her. If he wasn't going to say anything about last night then she decided to act as though nothing had ever happened.

She focused on the silver cases he shoved in the back compartment. "What's all this?"

"Weapons, supplies," he said as he picked another case and added it with the others.

Her gaze crept surreptitiously over him. He was fully clothed, but the image of his nude body had been branded in her mind. Beneath his attire she could make out his thick, corded muscles. She'd touched them—she remembered the caged power she'd felt.

Swallowing a lump in her throat, she moved forward and picked up the last case. "How far away is this witch we're going to see?" She handed it to him.

Nicholas accepted it. "My brother and I will do this alone, Daniela. You will remain here until we return."

She looked at him closely, noting he wore that stern expression she'd seen before. "What? How can you expect me to stay here? I told you, I'm not going to sit around waiting for something bad to happen."

"Things have changed within the past few hours and danger is sure to be lurking down the path we intend to take." He marched toward the side of the SUV and threw one of the rear doors open.

She pursued him. "Changed? What are you talking about?"

Reaching beneath the driver's seat, he pulled out a map. "While you slept I went to see the man we'd assumed was Sabbath. I confronted him and the situation escalated, and in his anger he underwent a transformation."

"He turned into a gargoyle?" She took in a breath of disbelief, and when he nodded she continued. "But how? I thought you said that you and your brother were the only ones who might be affected by whatever caused your transformation."

"I did, but there is dark sorcery afoot. What I told you was only speculation. Right now, we have no substantial evidence to link anyone to the crimes." He unfolded the map onto the back seat.

"And what about this guy who transformed into a gargoyle?" she asked. "Couldn't he be Sabbath?"

Nicholas traced a finger over the map. "It is a possibility. I continued my interrogation and he denied any involvement in the dark arts. It does not seem logical for one to inflict himself, but his transformation does not exempt him from suspicion. He will still be brought before the council."

Daniela took a moment to absorb everything he'd said. She understood it all, except his reason for forbidding her to come along.

He looked at her, his beautiful green eyes flickering with seriousness that nearly led her to believe that he cared for her. "If he is not Sabbath, then we have no idea where or when another attack will occur. Someone wants the Rune of Cythe and it seems he is prepared to do whatever necessary to obtain it."

Her determination didn't waver. "That someone also has my sister. I will fight at your side, Nicholas."

"No. You will remain here." He pulled a marker from the glove compartment and circled an area on the map.

"That's not fair," she protested. "What purpose would I be serving here?"

He spun on her. "You are the only one who knows the location of the rune. Should something happen to you it will be lost."

Her mouth fell open. "Is that all you care about? Your rune?"

She couldn't believe what she was hearing. It was glaringly obvious that last night had meant absolutely nothing to him. Had she been a fool to assume he'd been trying to protect her? Was it really the rune he was so worried about?

His eyes narrowed on her. "We will end this conversation here. My brother and I leave in forty-five minutes. I expect you to remain here until we return."

He didn't wait for her to respond. Instead, he turned and headed toward the door. Daniela glared after him. If she had a rock she would hurl it at his back. The side of him he'd shown her during the night was long gone. And in its place was the arrogant, stubborn bastard she'd come to know so well.

"As I said before, I'm not going to sit around

here wasting my time," she spat as Nicholas reached for the door. "If you can't take me where I need to be, then I'll find my way there myself."

Gritting her teeth, she snatched the map from the back seat and looked at the spot he'd circled. It was a city called Borsec. She assumed it was where the witch resided. She didn't know who she'd be looking for or what she could possibly learn from her, but she didn't know where else to start.

Nicholas paused at the door and turned to watch her. She sent him a rebellious glance and headed toward the back of the SUV. If things got heated, she'd need to defend herself. She yanked one of the silver cases flat and flicked it open. A set of sleek black guns grinned up at her. She snatched one up and checked to see if it was loaded.

When she turned around, Nicholas was standing behind her, looking severely annoyed. He snatched the gun from her hand and tossed it into the case.

Daniela tried to grab it. "What are you doing?"

He yanked the cargo door shut and pushed her up against it. Then, bracing an arm above her head, he glared down at her. Something dangerous flickered in his eyes.

"Why do you persist with this defiance?" he demanded.

"I'm not sure what kind of women you're accustomed to, but where I'm from we think for ourselves. We don't need to be constantly told what to do and when to do it."

"Not even if the instruction is for your own benefit?"

She gasped. "And just what gives you the impression that you know what's for my benefit?"

His voice was low when he spoke again. "You seem to have a difficult time determining it for yourself."

Daniela shook her head in disbelief and moved to step around him. "You arrogant son of a…"

Before she could complete her insult, she found herself pressed back up against the SUV. A second later Nicholas's hard mouth fell on her for a fevered kiss. Taken by surprise, she emitted a scream, but it was thoroughly muffled. She managed to resist him for an entire five seconds before she succumbed to the heated sensation that quickly swept over her.

The kiss was intoxicating. His large body sank into her and his strong hands moved over her curves. The memory of his lean form thrusting between her thighs was all too vivid and she felt herself becoming aroused.

She tried to resist it, of course. She wasn't about to let herself get sucked into him a second time. At least that's what she told herself. But, when Nicholas peeled himself away from her just enough to read her emotions, she offered no resistance.

That was all the encouragement he needed. He claimed her with another kiss and gripping her backside, lifted her against him. Shamefully, she wound her legs about him and her fingers got lost in his mane of dark hair. Nicholas carried her to the opened rear door of the SUV and lowered her onto the backseat.

Their kiss intensified and Nicholas's fingers moved to the zipper of her pants. A soft rasp followed and his fingers slipped into the opening. He made it abundantly clear exactly what he wanted as he began to stroke her softness under her panties. Daniela could not hold back a moan.

His fondling continued and one lean finger slipped into her, extracting another moan. Daniela pressed herself against his hand. She hated herself for responding to him this way. She knew that for him, intimacy was nothing more than a way to relieve himself. Yet, here she was, lying on her back with her legs spread wide beneath him. And she wanted him fiercely.

Nicholas raised her off the seat as he slipped her pants and underwear down to her knees. She quickly kicked off her boots, aiding him as he dragged her clothing down her legs. They were carelessly discarded on the back of the driver's seat and Nicholas looped his arms under her thighs and pulled her to the edge of the seat.

His smokey gaze held her in place. "You have two choices," he said in a very low voice.

Daniela suppressed a shudder as he traced his fingers up and down along her softness.

"You can reveal the location of the Rune of Cythe and I will allow you to accompany us. Or you can remain here." He waited.

Somehow she managed to weigh the options amidst the confusion in her head. It didn't take long to arrive at a decision. She needed to go with them. She knew that if she revealed the location of the rune she would be surrendering whatever leverage she had over him, but it was a chance she would have to take. Strangely, she felt she could trust Nicholas. It didn't seem likely that he would simply abandon her and her sister once he had what he wanted.

"I'll tell you where the rune is."

He nodded, but his expression remained the same. His attention dipped to the place where his fingers were lodged and with his free hand, he unzipped his pants, freeing his hard phallus.

The gentle pressure of his probing at her entrance sent her mind into another incoherent spin. Her arms enclosed around him as he lowered himself over her. And as he pressed into her, she welcomed every firm inch of him. The emotions she saw in him were illusions. They didn't exist, but were exacerbations of lust. Yet, in this moment she was happy to pretend that things were different. That Nicholas would find her to be more than just an object of desire. And when this was all over he'd want her for who she was.

Chapter 15

Entering Borsec was like stepping one hundred years into the past. With its quaint little cottages and dirt roads, it was a picturesque village that clung to the grassy hillside.

Nicholas surveyed the small wooden house that sat at the base of the hill. It was set away from the village and surrounded by a scattering of tall trees. They'd been directed there by a few of the villagers.

His attention spanned the area, seeking anything out of the ordinary. He'd learned from centuries of experience, that adversity could often be hidden in tranquility. Something within him warned that they would meet danger on their mission. Before leaving the mansion, he'd learned from his father that Stefan had failed to present himself before the Darcian Council. Then, upon a search of his home, it had been concluded that he was missing.

Nicholas had been more than surprised to learn that Stefan had also retained his ability to transform into a gargoyle. Initially, he'd been convinced only he and Simion had been affected because of the barrier spell they'd cast. But Stefan hadn't even attended that ceremony. How was it then that he presented with the same abilities?

During the long drive to the village, Nicholas had decided on two possible conclusions. One, because of Stefan's absence that night, he'd been freed from the curse, but the sorcery hadn't completely dissipated. And when new spells had started being performed in an effort to free Gabriel, Stefan had been susceptible to them. Or two, Stefan was the one responsible for the reckless witchcraft being performed, and in so doing, he'd reinstated his own abilities.

After his transformation, Stefan had admitted to Nicholas that he had sought out the assistance of witches, but only in an attempt to reverse what was happening to him. Nicholas had listened but had not relayed the fact that he shared the same dilemma, uncertain if Stefan could be trusted. And now with Stefan a fugitive, as he'd not reported to the Council after promising Nicholas he'd do so, he realized that he'd been wise to keep secret that information.

Simion began making his way down the hill and Nicholas sent Daniela a look over his shoulder. "Stay at my side," he said as he followed his brother.

He'd allowed Daniela to accompany them in exchange for the location of the rune. She'd confessed to burying it in a forest near Sighisoara. There'd been an exchange of trust between them. He'd had to accept her admission as the truth. He knew that if something happened to her, or if she found her sister and left spontaneously, all hope for recovering the rune would be lost.

She, on the other hand, had given up her leverage even with the looming possibility that he could've simply reneged on his promise to help her and focused his attentions on his pressing family matters. The faith she'd placed in him had enhanced his urge to find and rescue her little sister. It had shocked him to realize that at this point he was willing to go to any extent to set things right in her life. He had developed feelings for her, yes, but he knew that his devotion was due mostly to pity. Or so he told himself. Danicla's life had been hard. It was time some good fortune came her way. Her admission had also served to diminish Simion's contempt toward her, and his brother had not objected to her coming along.

As they approached the house, Nicholas could see the figure of a woman hunched over what appeared to be a small vegetable garden. They paused before the wooden gate that was partially concealed by an overgrowth of shrubbery and she turned to look at them. If his father had been correct, she was called Adela and had once been the pupil of the witch who'd bound Gabriel's soul into the runes.

"Good day," Simion greeted her. "We are…"

"I know who you are," Adela interjected.

She appeared to be in her late sixties, but was hundreds of years old, so they'd been told. She was dressed in a knitted green sweater and a long skirt, and her hair was covered with a scarf that was fastened beneath her chin. She advanced, wiping her hands on her apron.

"I exchanged words with your father," she said. "I have been awaiting your arrival. Please, come inside."

They followed her into the house and were greeted by the subtle tunes of wind chimes. Simion ducked his head as he entered, but Nicholas saw the colorful chimes too late. There were about fifteen of them strung above the doorway and they chorused wildly as he passed through them.

Adela laughed mischievously. "Ignore them. They let me know when spirits enter my home."

She led them to a modest dining room that was dominated by a long wooden table. One side was neatly arranged with metal plates and cutlery, while the other side was cluttered with candles, empty glass jars with their necks wrapped with twine, and a collection of colorful ornate bottles.

"Please, sit." She motioned toward the table which had been set for three. "I was not expecting so many visitors, but you can sit in my place, dear."

Daniela smiled graciously at Adela and moved to the head of the table. Nicholas pulled the chair for her and took the seat to her right. Simion sat opposite him.

Adela disappeared into a room Nicholas assumed was the kitchen. Wonderful smells poured out and he could hear running water then the clanking of dishes within.

Simion leaned forward on the table. "Do you think she can be trusted?"

Nicholas nodded. "Father instructed us to visit her and I trust his judgment."

He exchanged a look with Daniela. He could tell that she was still not too pleased with the purpose of their mission—to find a way to deactivate the runes. She was still afraid that if they were able to achieve such a thing and her sister's captor found out, the situation would be out of her control. He understood her fear, and would do whatever was in his power to deliver her sister from the kidnapper before any potential leaks could reach them.

Adela returned with a large oval tray laden with bread, a bottle of wine and a steaming ceramic dish. She placed it on the table.

"This is my favorite. It's called *sarmale*," she said as she served them.

She'd also brought another plate for herself and she sat to eat with them.

"So you wish to know more about the rune," she said and the jovial light in her eyes simmered to seriousness.

Nicholas nodded. "If our father has not already told you, you should know that the Rune of Moloch has been stolen. It is one of the runes Agatha used in the binding spell she performed centuries ago. And now, our adversary is after its twin and his intentions are more than clear. He will attempt to awaken our uncle and his followers."

"I see," Adela said. "And what would you ask of me?"

Nicholas looked at his brother and it was Simion who supplied the answer. "We have come to you with the hope of finding a way to strip the runes of their powers."

Adela sighed softly and lowered her fork. "Knowledge of runes is not something that is heavily focused upon as it is a dying method in the craft. Nevertheless, everything in sorcery can be manipulated, with the right spells, of course."

"So there is a way?" Simion asked.

Adela took a sip of her wine. "There is always a way. But it is as I said, the right spell must be used. I alone do not possess these abilities. The ancient spell books that governed such things have been lost for many years."

Nicholas could feel the hope fast leaving him. "And there are absolutely no other spells that can be substituted?"

"Perhaps," Adela admitted. "But the process of trial and error could prove to be more detrimental than actually releasing the beast that remains in captivity."

She was right. Nicholas's own transformation was no doubt a result of sorcery cast in trial and error. Complicating things with uncertainty was definitely not an option. It seemed they'd run out of choices. The runes couldn't be destroyed or deactivated.

Simion exhaled a heavy breath. "Is there no other option?" he asked.

Adela set her glass down. "There is one way, but if you choose this, no spell will be able to undo it." Her gaze was intense as she combed the faces of those present.

Nicholas's eyes narrowed in curiosity. "What is it?"

Again she sent her gaze about the table. "The only way you can assure that the statues are never resurrected is by destroying them."

Silence crept into the room and Nicholas exchanged looks with Simion. By the expression on his brother's face, he knew that they shared the same thought. There was a chance that their father wouldn't agree to this method, for Lord Victor still had many regrets about what he'd done to his own brother. For centuries Lord Victor had blamed himself for what Gabriel had become, since it was he who had brought the curse upon their family. To think that their father would simply agree to completely destroy

Gabriel was foolish. But their father had stated that destroying the statues would be done as a last resort, and Nicholas felt they'd arrived at that point of desperation.

Simion's head fell. "And if we do this and the runes are still broken, what will happen to the souls within them?"

"Without hosts it will be as in death. The souls will be released into the spirit world."

Daniela's attention snapped to Nicholas. It was obvious that she was waiting for his response. What Adela described could be considered murder and he didn't want to give Daniela the impression that life was insignificant to him. She'd seen him kill before; if he could avoid it, he wouldn't want her to witness it again.

Simion pinned Nicholas with a stare and he understood. They'd been handed a solution and they had no choice but to make use of it. The statues would have to be destroyed.

Adela stood and moved toward the brick fireplace. A small flame burned within, warming the room. She knelt and removed a brick from the wall at the base of the fireplace, revealing a small compartment. She reached in and withdrew an item that was wrapped in a length of haggard cloth. She returned to the table and handed it to Nicholas.

"What is this?" he asked.

"Should you be too late," her voice was barely audible as she spoke. "Use it."

Simion's head came up slowly and he and Daniela watched as Nicholas carefully unfolded the cloth. A small bronze dagger with a hilt engraved with Ananovian symbols lay within.

Disappointment weighed heavily on him. "A lovely blade, but I fail to see how it will help."

Adela reached forward with both hands and removed the dagger from its wrapping. "Ah, it is no more a simple dagger than the runes are worthless stones. Even you should know that in sorcery, things are often more than they seem."

"What is it then?" Nicholas watched as she brought the weapon up to her eye level.

She rotated it, examining the inscriptions that Nicholas now realized spilled onto the blade. "It is my most powerful return spell. I am often taunted by spirits and I use these spells to cast them back into the pits from which they came. They can also be used to reverse spells."

Simion reached for the blade and she passed it to him. "How is it used?" he asked.

"You must plunge it into the flesh of the beast. But know this—it can only be used once, and it will only be effective during or shortly after the resurrection takes place."

Daniela, who'd been silent throughout the conversation, spoke up. "It's only one dagger, though. There are twelve statues."

Adela nodded regretfully. "I have no others like it, and it would take at least a fortnight for me to fashion the quantity you require. You see, a combination of spells must be carefully and sequentially integrated into the dagger for it to be effective. Therefore, you must use this one where and when it is most needed."

Chapter 16

Nicholas barely recognized the grounds of Fagara Castle. The land was overrun by weeds and vines, heavy trees loomed about, fighting off the pale moonlight. It had been nearly two hundred years since he'd last been there, yet he could vividly recall the night Gabriel and his followers had been brought in off the battlefield. Their tortured screams lingered in the air, filling the cavity of time.

Simion paused at his side. He traced his flashlight along the dilapidated ramparts above.

"So much has changed," he said.

Nicholas grunted in agreement. Uneasiness

crept over him and he drew his gun. He sent Daniela a look that warned her to be on her guard. Their gazes held for a moment and even in the darkness, he could read the havoc of emotions that doubtlessly tortured her. She was afraid, yet courage and determination resonated amidst her trepidation. She was truly a strong, beautiful and unique woman. Much like him, she faced her fears and adversaries with an unfaltering boldness. And this he admired. With his eyes, he sent her a silent promise—he'd allow no harm to befall her.

Together, the three of them advanced up the stone steps that led into the castle's front entrance. The door had long decayed, leaving a yawning archway. Nicholas was first to enter while Simion lingered in the rear, scanning the shadows.

Upon entering the foyer, Nicholas realized that the once beautiful domed ceiling had all but caved in. A gaping hole remained, permitting a scant view of the moon through the branches overhead. The majority of the walls had also crumbled and the second floor was completely gone, leaving the rooms open to the night. And as the trees parted, the starlit sky became visible overhead. The ground was also covered with grass and weeds, yet he managed to locate the passage that led to the dungeon.

"This way," he said.

Daniela and Simion followed him. The glow from their flashlights cast shadows on the walls, obscuring Nicholas's perceptions of what lay ahead. He held his gun ready for anything, but he wasn't prepared for what he found at the end of the passage. The thick wall that he himself had helped to erect had been destroyed, and the stairway that led down into the dungeon could be seen.

The pounding of his heart wasn't enough to subdue the warning bells that went off in his head. Were they too late? Had Gabriel already been awakened?

He shot Simion and Daniela a glance over his

shoulder. "The barrier is gone," he said before ducking in the portal.

He cocked his gun as he descended the stairway. At the bottom, his fear was realized. The twelve statues were gone.

Simion stormed into the chamber. "Who could've done this?" he asked, furious. Daniela wore a worried expression. "We're too late, aren't we?"

Nicholas trailed the light over the dust-laden floor. "So it would seem." He noted that there were only human footprints in the dust.

He frowned. There was no way the gargoyles could've flown out of there, and there were no signs that the statues had been removed through the entrance. He wondered if Stefan had been right. Perhaps the twelve gargoyles had become human with the rest of the clan. That, or some sort of witchcraft had been used.

Simion crouched to the floor and studied the tracks, as well. "It has been about two days since whatever happened here took place."

Nicholas's discontent rose. If his brother was right then there was a chance that Gabriel and those loyal to him had already been awoken. But without the use of the second rune there was no telling what sort of mindless entities had been brought into the world. And with so much time elapsed, the dagger that Adela had given them was useless.

A sound emerged from outside. It was unmistakable—the steady beating of wings. One thought clamored in his mind: Gabriel had returned or had never left his place of captivity!

Simion stripped the crossbow from his back and they ran up the stairway. A large form was silhouetted by the moon. It hovered in the sky above, its massive wings fluidly caressing the night air.

Without taking his eyes from the gargoyle, Nicholas reached for Daniela and gently eased her behind them. If the one above them was truly Gabriel then that could only mean that eleven others lurked about. A fight was inevitable.

Nicholas aimed his gun and beside him, his brother brought his crossbow up.

"Show yourself," Nicholas said loudly.

"It is as I thought," came a heavy voice. "You and your brother have betrayed the Drakon Clan."

Daniela spoke then. "Who is he?" she asked.

Instantly, Nicholas recognized the voice. The gargoyle wasn't Gabriel, but Stefan. "He is the one we suspect is Sabbath," he replied.

Stefan continued. "It seems my suspicions were correct. I do not know how I missed it before. You and your brother are the only ones Lord Drakon would ever trust with his secrets."

Nicholas's eyes narrowed on him. He wondered if Stefan was really blaming them for everything that happened or trying to provide a distraction.

Simion kept his crossbow aimed. "You are

wanted before the Darcian Council. Surrender yourself."

Stefan's laugh was quick and derisive. "And be brought to trial for the crimes that you two have committed? I think not. I must commend you on your cleverness, though. I would imagine that deceiving Lord Victor, and doing so right in front of his eyes, is no easy task." He swooped upward and perched on the peak of a wall.

Stefan's attention flitted to Daniela. "And who is she? The witch who has been aiding you?"

Nicholas's gun followed him. "We are not the ones responsible for this. Tell me, what reason do you have for being here?"

"I have been following you since you left my home this morning. I see now that I was right to do so. I have all the proof I need to implicate you and clear my name."

An impatient growl escaped his brother and Nicholas glanced at Simion just in time to see his finger case on the trigger of the crossbow.

"I grow tired of your nonsense," Simion barked. "Come with us willingly or you will be taken by force."

In one fluid movement Stefan sprang into the air, reached over his shoulder and swung a large crossbow toward them. "You will fall dead before the arrow left your bow," he gritted out.

Instinctively, Nicholas cocked his gun. Stefan, like Simion, had fought in many wars. He wasn't sure how skilled he was with a bow, but he wasn't about to risk losing his brother. He would kill Stefan on the spot if he had to.

"We found the wall of the dungeon destroyed. Where are the twelve statues?" Nicholas asked. "What have you done with them?"

Stefan said nothing for a moment and when he spoke his voice was laced with confusion. "I know nothing of what you speak."

Nicholas would've accused him a second time, but Daniela gripped him on the arm, drawing his attention.

"Nicholas, what's going on?" She pointed.

He followed her direction and his breathing paused. From where they stood they could see beyond the dilapidated castle walls and into the main courtyard. A large hole had been ripped into the darkness. Its circumference was at least ten feet wide. It blotted out the trees behind it and its center wavered as if draped in a thick curtain of smoke.

"Witchcraft," was all Nicholas managed to say.

The spectacle also drew Simion and Stefan's attentions and they all gazed on with mounting consternation. The sound of hooves emerged from the blackness and a second later, a huge and glossy black stallion stepped through. Atop it sat a woman, her poise regal and proud. Also garbed in black, she sported a massive silver headdress. On either side of her horse, two other women emerged on foot.

Daniela's grip tightened on Nicholas's arm. "That's them, the witches who attacked me!"

Nicholas guessed that the woman upon the

horse was the leader of the Raba witch clan. Her name eluded him, but he had heard of her. She was a callous bitch whose lust for power was incessant. Her own husband had died at her hands—an act of self-defense, or so she'd claimed. And she'd wasted no time in taking up his staff as sovereign.

Simion cast a look up at Stefan. "What manner of sorcery have you brought down upon us?"

Stefan shook his head slowly. "It is not my doing."

The figures of about twelve men also appeared out of the gateway. They were tall and wore long, black warrior kilts. Their muscled chests were bare save for the tattoos that covered their skin. Their faces were partially concealed by bands of cloth that were wound about their mouths and their long dark hair fell nearly to their waist.

Raba warlocks, Nicholas thought with distaste. He'd encountered their kind before. They were men renowned for their fighting skill, and they'd posed a great challenge to the Ananovian witch clan during the great wars. They gleaned their strength and speed from magic crystals. It was through their intrusion that the Ananovians had sought to form an alliance with the gargoyles.

The portal snapped shut and the two witches on foot raised their hands simultaneously to point toward Daniela. Their lips began to move in unison, spilling forth an ancient spell. A riveting wall of fire blazed forward, lighting the atmosphere and searing everything in its path. The warlocks advanced, racing forward and leaping over fallen slabs of stones. Several of them held scythes.

Nicholas's party fell back immediately. Simion began releasing a series of arrows, but the warlocks were too fast. They dodged the projectiles with ease.

"How did they find me?" Daniela gasped.

Nicholas passed his gun to her and motioned

toward a pillar that had collapsed. "Conceal yourself," he ordered.

She accepted the gun and cocked it. "No! I said I would fight at your side." Without waiting for his approval, she raised the gun and began firing at the advancing warlocks.

Nicholas ripped his jacket off and summoned the darkness within him. His pulse quickened and his body began to morph. The roar he emitted as he became a gargoyle was born of the agony that pulsed through him and his anger toward those who dared to harm Daniela.

The warlocks descended upon them, slashing madly with their scythes. Nicholas sprung into the air as one of them made a swing for his legs. He swept down and gripped the man by the throat, lifting him high off the ground before discarding him. Stefan had joined the skirmish. He fought like a well-honed warrior, evading attacks and laying flat those who opposed him.

Nicholas didn't let Daniela out of his sight.

She'd resorted to using martial arts to defend herself. On several occasions he had to interject and ward off an attacker, but otherwise Daniela fought with the grace and speed of a well-trained warrior.

Simion's scream echoed throughout the ruins. Nicholas's attention was drawn to his brother, who lay on the ground, gripping his arm. He'd been injured and a warlock stood above him with a massive silver scythe in his grip. Nicholas moved to aid Simion, but was rammed off his feet. Together he and the warlock who'd attacked him went scraping across the earth, ripping up the weeds and shattering the low remnants of brick walls.

With both hands, the warlock raised a long knife above his head and was about to plunge it into Nicholas's flesh. A gunshot rang out and the warlock froze. A trickle of blood oozed from his nose and he collapsed to one side. A few feet behind him, Daniela stood with the gun. She met Nicholas's eyes for a brief second, relaying the same message he'd given her before: she wasn't about to let anything happen to him.

Nicholas sprang to his feet and found his brother again. Only Simion had released the beast that had been stirring within him for months. He too had become a gargoyle.

The fight continued and victory began to sway in their favor. The leader of the Raba clan raised a hand and called out an order in an ancient tongue. The twins at her side raised their crystals and began chanting. Immediately, the portal was reopened. She spun her black horse around and with a final venomous glance, she passed through it. Her minions followed, retreating with the same speed with which they had attacked.

Nicholas leaped into the air and flew toward the portal. It snapped shut just before he could enter. In a rage, he gripped one of the injured warlocks by the hair and wound it about his fist. He yanked the man's head backward and drew the knife from his boot, placing it against his throat.

"Who has hired you to do this?" he asked through barred teeth.

The warlock laughed, spurting blood from his lips. "The prophecy…will soon be fulfilled," he choked out.

Nicholas frowned at him. "What prophecy do you speak of?"

Again the warlock laughed. Nicholas yanked his head backward another few inches. "Answer me!" he barked, just as the warlock slipped into unresponsiveness.

"That is enough," Simion's voice invaded his mind.

He looked up. Simion was approaching him while Stefan watched from one side. At the very rear, Daniela looked on with wide eyes. With the aid of the fires that still burned about them, he could read the fear on her face. He released the man and stood. He'd never felt such pulsing rage before. He knew it had quite a bit to do with Daniela and her missing sister. There seemed to be no hope of finding answers. He felt free to assume that Stefan wasn't behind everything that had happened, but that took them back to square one.

Simion paused next to him. "We need to return to the estate. These matters require more than just our own attention now." He turned to Stefan. "Please. Allow us to extend our apologies for doubting you."

Nicholas inclined his head in agreement. Stefan still wore an expression of surprise. Nicholas guessed that he'd never expected them to be gargoyles, as well.

Stefan nodded. "It is in the past. Right now we must focus strictly upon remedying the situation at hand."

He was right. There was simply too much at stake to waste their efforts worrying over misplaced accusations. Nicholas motioned for Daniela to quickly join them. As soon as he'd taken his attention from her, he was forced to look again. His brows began to bend and a cry rose within his throat.

"Daniela!"

Behind her, partially masked in the shadow of a wall, a black hole had opened. She'd only taken two steps when two tentacle-like whiffs of smoke snaked out.

Fear like none he'd ever experienced before possessed him and he sprang into the air. "Run!" he screamed.

But it was too late. One whiff of smoke wrapped itself about her neck and the other encircled her waist. It was soon joined by others. She struggled madly, gasping for air as she tried to pry her neck free. But it was to no avail. She was pulled to the earth and her eyes met Nicholas's one last time. She reached for him, gasping his name silently into the night. And then she was gone.

Nicholas landed on the ground just as the last flailing tips of the smoke crept back into the shadows. An anguished roar tore through his throat and he crumpled to his knees. His head fell into his hands and he cursed himself. He'd vowed to protect her. The mere thought of the tortures she'd have to endure at the hands of those who sought the runes sent a wave of agony over him. Fury filled his eyes as he lifted them to the shadow into which she'd disappeared, and his breathing came in heavy gasps. He'd be damned if he allowed anyone to take her away from him. She'd become his amusement, his desire, his equal and his purpose. And with certainty, he realized now that he loved her.

Chapter 17

The sound of water lapping against rocks woke her. Daniela moaned and eased her eyes open. Her head ached and she was cold. She blinked against the darkness that greeted her. As her eyes adjusted, she could see that she was in some sort of shack. Crates were stacked against one wall and on the other side a very narrow slit had been cut into the wall. It permitted a short beam of moonlight in.

Daniela stood and steadied herself before heading toward the little window. She extended her wrist beneath it and checked her watch. It was 9:50 p.m., which meant she'd been there for about one hour. She remembered everything that had occurred at the castle ruins. She could also recall the cry that Nicholas had emitted as she'd been forced into the darkness. At this moment she yearned for him, for the security he presented. She was afraid.

Tiptoeing, she spied through the opening. A beautiful lake lay on the other side. The reflection of the moon danced on its surface as it rippled lazily. Daniela could tell that she was below the ground level, for grass and shrubs partially obscured her vision.

She was momentarily tempted to cry out for help, but thought against it. No one was in sight and she didn't want to alert any of the wrong people that she was awake. And so she turned to study the room. A heavy wooden door seemed to be the only entrance. She went to it and gripped the handle. A few tries revealed that it was locked.

She felt her hair for any pins that might've survived the bedlam she'd endured. To her delight she located one. Kneeling, she felt for the keyhole and immediately deduced that it was an old-fashioned lock. She sighed. Without any substantial light to aid her, picking it was definitely going to take a miracle. She closed her eyes and slipped the pin in. It might prove to be easier if she tried to feel her way through it.

She was still kneeling behind the door when she heard movement on the other side. Light seeped in from beneath the door and the jingle of keys could be heard. Daniela jumped up and backed toward the rear of the room.

The door opened and the twin Raba witches entered. One bore a single candle. They stepped to the side and a man entered. He wore a black hooded cloak that billowed around him. Draped about his neck was a heavy necklace from which a golden ram's head dangled. His face was moderately obscured by the shadow of the black hood, but there was an air about him that made her wary.

"Ah, our little thief," he spoke.

Daniela frowned at him. "Who are you?"

She knew the answer before her question was complete. He was the man who'd hired her and the one who held her sister. He was Sabbath.

He laughed softly. "The first day I saw you I knew who you were. It was the look in your eyes—the discomfort. But that wasn't the time to confront you. So I had you followed." He brought his hands together in a clap. "And here you are. And now my dear, you will tell me where the Rune of Cythe is hidden."

"Where's my sister?" Daniela blurted. She wasn't giving up any information until she knew that Elaina was safe.

Sabbath motioned toward the twin without the candle and she disappeared from the room. A moment later she returned with another person. Daniela's heart stopped then started to beat rapidly again. Elaina was alive.

"Daniela!" Elaina started crying and tried to run to her, but was held firmly by the witch.

Elaina was still dressed in her pale blue pajamas and fuzzy, alien bedroom slippers. She was dirty, but otherwise looked unharmed.

Tears welled in Daniela's eyes and she pinned Sabbath with a hard look. "Let her go," she gritted out.

"Where is the rune?"

She hesitated. There was still the possibility that she and Elaina would be killed once the rune was found, but what other choice did she have? If she resisted she was sure they would threaten Elaina's well-being to gain her compliance. At least by admitting the location, she would be able to buy them some time. Nicholas would find them. Of this she was sure.

"Release her to me," she told Sabbath. "And I'll tell you anything you want to know."

Sabbath only watched her for a moment, then he motioned to the witch who held Elaina. She let her go and Elaina raced toward Daniela.

"I'll hold you to that," Sabbath told her. "And if you try to deceive me in any way your sister's blood will be on your hands."

Daniela pulled Elaina into an embrace and held her tightly. Elaina began to sob into her shoulder. "Everything's going to be okay," she said soothingly.

Elaina looked up at her with tears streaking her cheeks. "Let's get out of here. I want to go home."

Daniela kissed her forehead. "We will. Just hold on a little longer." She sent Sabbath a hateful look. "Why are you doing this?"

"Why?" He began sauntering toward them. "Because it's time I claimed my birthright. I should be leader of my clan. Too long have I taken orders and held my tongue."

He paused before them and stripped the hood from his head. Daniela gasped in disbelief.

He continued. "Too long have I shared my inheritance with those who should've been gone a long time ago. Too long have I wilted in Victor Drakon's shadow."

Daniela's arms tightened about Elaina and she fought the sickening feeling that was churning in her stomach. She couldn't believe that Sabbath was none other than Andrew Drakon.

They'd decided that there was no time to return to the mansion. With Daniela stolen, Nicholas knew that Sabbath's next move would be to retrieve the Rune of Cythe. He'd revealed its hiding place to Simion and Stefan and they'd made their way there without delay. The way to Sighisoara was a long one and they'd decided to fly to save time. Once there, they would wait in concealment until someone arrived to retrieve the rune, and then they hoped be led to the place where Daniela and the twelve statues were being kept.

He only prayed that their efforts weren't in vain, for it seemed the Raba witches had developed their own quick modes of transportation. Gateways had never been used in the past and it would make tracking them impossible.

Simion's voice invaded his thoughts. "Are you

sure the girl spoke the truth? Is this where the rune is buried?"

They were perched high above the ground in the trees. Nicholas surveyed the large moss-covered boulder that sat near the center of the clearing. From his vantage point he could make out no sign that the ground had been manipulated. Yet he held fast to his faith in Daniela.

He nodded. "It is. We have only to wait."

Stefan, who was on another branch a few feet away, motioned toward them and pointed toward the highway that was visible through the trees. A car was pulling to the wayside, its headlights sweeping through the trees. It came to a stop and the engine purred off.

Nicholas watched as the doors opened. Instantly, he saw Daniela. His heart constricted and he had to steel himself to remain where he was. Three others exited the car; a man, a woman and a teenage girl. The woman was one of the Raba twins and she held on to the girl. Nicholas guessed that the girl was Daniela's little sister. The man looked to be nothing more than a servant.

With Daniela in the lead, they moved down the sloping hill that flattened out into the clearing. Nicholas's gaze stayed on Daniela as she passed beneath him. She looked scared and uncertain, but he could tell that she was being quite brave for her sister. He wanted nothing more than to go down and save her, but now wasn't the time to act. Sabbath wasn't present and the statues had yet to be recovered.

Daniela motioned toward the boulder. "The rune is buried next to it."

The witch jerked her head toward the boulder. "Retrieve it," she said.

It was then that Nicholas noticed the knife in the witch's hand. It was pressed up against the girl's rib cage.

Daniela moved forward and kneeled next to the boulder. She began digging in the soil and after a minute, she pulled out what appeared to be a bundle of newspaper. The witch nodded at the man and he advanced and took the bundle from Daniela's hands. Carefully, he unraveled it to reveal the Rune of Cythe inside. A grin crept to his face as he held it up for inspection.

Nicholas exchanged looks with Simion and Stefan. They were risking much by allowing them to walk away with the second rune, but there was no other way. There were still mysteries that needed to be solved.

The group on the ground began making their way back toward the car. Nicholas watched Daniela. He wished that there was a way he could let her know that he was with her. But he couldn't. The slightest indication that something was amiss could completely foil their plans. And so he maintained his position until the car crawled back onto the highway.

No words were exchanged after that. It was clear what needed to be done. In unison, they sprang from the branches and took to the sky, disappearing into the darkness overhead.

Chapter 18

Nicholas studied the mound of rock that cascaded down the cliff and disappeared into the water. They'd followed the vehicle to this point, and while the car remained parked at the edge of the cliff, its occupants were nowhere to be found. There was nothing for miles and thus they'd quickly concluded that the cliff was far more than it appeared to be.

It was Stefan who'd discovered the access to the cave that was near the base of the cliff. They'd returned to their human forms and now stood just within the entrance. The antechamber was vast. Its walls were smooth and the ceiling was decorated with hundreds of pointed stalactites. The room branched off into two passages, each lit by a torch that had been fastened to the wall.

Nicholas motioned to the right. "I will follow this path."

Simion and Stefan nodded and headed for the opposing one. Nicholas drew his gun and began walking. He moved quickly, his eyes and ears missing nothing. If Daniela was somewhere inside this cave then he was going to find her. He didn't care how long it took or who he'd have to face. He wasn't leaving without her.

As he came to the end of the passage, the sound of voices could be heard. He eased into another passage and saw an opening at the end. He made his way toward it. Beyond it, a flight of crudely fashioned stairs gave access to a wide chamber. Fires burned around the room in metal fire pits, casting light on the occupants within.

Nicholas slipped into the shadows at the top of the stairway and took a moment to come to terms with what he saw. Eleven gargoyle statues stood in a row on a raised platform of stone, while the figure of Gabriel had been placed at the very back of the room upon a low pedestal. A gaping hole in the wall permitted a view of the moon as it sank lower in the sky.

A hooded figure stood before the statue, watching as one of the Raba witch twins carved a symbol around it. Five men in suits also stood back to observe.

Movement resounded from one end of the chamber and Nicholas's attention was drawn to another passageway. Light spilled from it and soon the leader of the Raba clan sauntered in. Behind her, the second twin followed with Daniela's sister, who was sobbing uncontrollably.

Nicholas's body tensed as another huddle of shadows began to pour from the doorway. Four Raba warlocks emerged, and, as he'd suspected, Daniela was among them. Her hands were bound with chains and the man who held them yanked her forward. Nicholas could feel a wave of heat slowly climbing over him and his joints began to ache. He flexed the muscles of his neck, suppressing the demon that fought for release.

He watched as Daniela was placed in the center of another symbol that had been drawn on the ground. A tall wooden stake had been erected within it as well, and it was to this that she was fastened.

The Raba leader cast her glance about the room. "Sabbath, it appears that everything is in order."

The cloaked figure turned to face her. "Excellent. Shall we begin?"

"I trust you will not forget our arrangement," she said. "My services are not free. Once you have what you want, the Book of Spirits is mine."

"Of course, Magdelene," Sabbath agreed. "It will be no more use to me."

Nicholas felt the blood drain from his face

and his brows sank into a deep and incredulous scowl. The voice he'd heard was all too familiar to him. His cousin Andrew was Sabbath. Andrew, who for years had taken up the task of conducting business for the Drakon family as Lord Victor had been unable to do so as a gargoyle. The mention of the Book of Spirits was also disturbing, as it was one of the lost spell books that Adela had mentioned. They were a collection of incantations that had been compiled over centuries. The spells had been conjured by the greatest warlocks and witches in history. It was during the time the books were used that the world had fallen into darkness. Spells were cast out of anger and lust for vengeance, and abominations had been formed.

Yet as the centuries passed, the dark magic had been contained and the books had been hidden away. How Andrew had come to possess one of them, Nicholas couldn't even begin to imagine.

Sabbath's attention turned to Gabriel's form again. "Are you sure this will work?" he asked.

The witch's chin went up a notch. "Most certain." She motioned toward an altar and from where Nicholas stood, he could see the two runes resting upon it. "Once the runes are broken, Gabriel's soul will be placed into the host."

They looked toward Daniela and Magdelene continued. "Simultaneously, your soul must also be removed and you will possess Gabriel's body."

"There are twelve souls within these runes," Sabbath stated. "How can you be sure that the right one will be exchanged?"

"It is sorcery, my dear," she replied. "The spell will be adjusted so that his name is used. Only his soul will be commanded into the host."

Sabbath looked at Daniela again. "And the girl, what happens to her once Gabriel's soul enters her body?"

Magdelene motioned toward the twins. One of them moved to stand behind the altar where the runes lay, while the other took a position by an altar near Daniela. Upon it was a heavy spell book.

"Essentially, if her soul is not strong enough, and I suspect it is not, she will die," Magdelene supplied impassively.

Nicholas had heard enough. He cocked his gun and headed down the stairway. "Andrew!"

All eyes turned to him and his gun came up at any who moved. One of the men dressed in a suit was about to reach into his jacket and Nicholas fired at him. The bullet struck the wall, but had been close enough to still the man's actions. It hadn't been Nicholas's intention to wound him, because he was grossly outnumbered. He fired the shot with the hopes of alerting his brother and Stefan. And until they found him, he would focus on getting Daniela and her sister out of there.

As he neared the bottom of the stairs, Andrew stripped the hood from his head. Surprise was evident on his face, but it was quickly subdued and replaced with a hard expression. Nicholas cast a look at Daniela, who watched him with a fusion of relief and fear.

"What is the meaning of this?" Magdelene demanded. Andrew raised a hand, quieting her.

"I commend you," Andrew said. "I didn't think you would make it this far."

Nicholas swung his gun on him. "You have betrayed our clan to satisfy your own greed for power."

A reflection of guilt registered in Andrew's eyes. "To want what is rightfully mine is hardly greed, Nicholas. You've been so eager to give up your life as a gargoyle, you didn't know what you had. The strength. The superiority. Now it's my turn."

A burning anger took hold of Nicholas. "And you would risk the safety of your family and of the innocent people in this world to achieve this?"

Andrew turned away and with adoration his eyes gazed upon the statue of Gabriel. "It was never my intention, but this is my last resort. You must understand that I have tried other spells to transform myself, but they were useless. But in Gabriel's body, I will be everything that I've always dreamed of."

"So you are the one who has been tampering with sorcery."

He nodded. "The Book of Spirits has many spells. Finding the correct one is an immense task. And in case you're wondering how I managed to find the book, I have spent over a year tracing the lineage of the witch to whom the book had been entrusted. And finally, I found her descendant. To her, the book had held no value and she'd kept it tucked away in the attic. Under the guise of an antiques dealer, I simply waltzed in and she exchanged it for a small fee of five hundred dollars."

Nicholas didn't appreciate the self-satisfied tone to his voice. "And are you aware that your interference has brought the effects of the curse back upon us?"

Andrew returned his attention to him. "So I've heard, but you should be grateful. It's because of those abilities that you are still alive."

Nicholas didn't deny the truth to those words, but it did nothing to change the fact that what Andrew had done was wrong. And they had yet to learn if the curse would take on its full effect. If it did, their lives would return to the hell it had been before.

Andrew sauntered forward until he stood within a few feet of Nicholas. "I will give you a chance to walk out of here and return to your life."

"Release the prisoners," was Nicholas's only reply. His primary concern was getting Daniela and her sister out of there before things got out of control.

"I'm afraid I cannot do that. I need a host to complete this spell, but you may leave with one of them."

Nicholas looked from Daniela to her little sister. What Andrew asked was completely out of the question. He'd made a promise to Daniela to see her and Elaina to safety and he intended to keep that promise.

"Release them and I will be your host," Nicholas offered.

For what seemed to be a long time, Andrew looked at him in disbelief. Then reluctantly, he nodded. "Very well."

He motioned to the men in the suits and two of them moved forward. Nicholas didn't wait for them. He marched toward Daniela and gazed down at her. Tears welled in her eyes and the pain he saw there was unmatched by anything he'd ever experienced before.

"Why are you doing this?" she asked.

He slipped the gun into her pocket. His eyes searched her face, memorizing it. She was so lovely. And he was willing to give his life for her. One of his hands moved to encircle her slender waist and he lowered his head. Their lips met for a soft and tender kiss. It wasn't driven by lust, but by the emotions that had urged him to find her.

The sounds of her chains being released echoed somewhere within the haze of his mind and he felt her arms lift to embrace him. She held him tightly. Their lips parted and he took another moment to just look at her.

"I want you to take your sister and leave this place," he told her.

She shook her head. "What about you?"

He brought a hand up and brushed a tear from her cheek. "There is no need to worry. Now do not waste any more time. Leave this place."

He stepped away from her and his arms were immediately seized by two men. They brought him up against the stake and chained him in place. He watched as Daniela ran to retrieve her sister. They headed up the stairway, but before she left the room, she turned back. Their eyes met one last time before she slipped out. Relief seeped into him. Daniela was safe.

"Add another length of chain," Andrew ordered.

The two men complied and Nicholas was soon wrapped in several thick chains. Andrew nodded at Magdelene and she motioned to the twin who stood nearest to Nicholas. The young woman began chanting from the thick spell book before her: the Book of Spirits.

Andrew moved to stand in the center of a symbol on the floor. It had been positioned next to the statue of Gabriel. Magdelene gestured toward the second twin, who hovered above the runes.

"Break the stones," Magdelene instructed.

The young woman raised her hands above her head. She held a large rock between them, but before she could bring it down, a loud crashing sound shook the entire room. All eyes were drawn to the pile of crumbled stone that lay at the bottom of the platform. Ten statues remained. Simion and Stefan hovered above them all, their large wings ripping through the air.

"Traitor!" Simion growled, his attention on Andrew.

Andrew realized that his plan was about to be foiled and he gestured wildly to his men. "Stop them!"

They pulled their guns and started firing. The Raba warlocks followed suit and made ready to attack. Simion and Stefan dodged the bullets with ease, swooping about the large room and taking out their enemies one at a time.

This was all Nicholas had been waiting for. He clenched his fist and began to strain against the chains that bound him.

Magdelene quickly retreated to the rear wall. "Break the runes!" she shouted.

The young Raba witch with the rock complied. She lifted her arms again and brought the rock down hard on the runes. A sudden burst of light shot out from beneath the rock. She lifted it, and what appeared to be coils of gossamer smoke rose from the shattered remains.

"The spell!" Andrew shouted at her sister and the other young witch began chanting anew.

At this point, Nicholas let loose the restraint on the dark creature within him. He began to transform and the chains broke away. Free now, he emitted a fierce roar and sprang into the air. It was time to end this.

With Elaina in tow, Daniela reached the exit of the cave. Behind them the sounds of gunfire and screams could be heard. It should've felt good to be free and to have her sister safely returned to her. But it didn't. She thought of Nicholas, who'd been left behind to endure whatever fate, only moments ago, had been her own. His sacrifice for her and Elaina had touched her deeply. No one had ever cared enough to risk anything for them, let alone their own life.

She paused at the exit, torn between the desire to get her sister as far away from there as possible and the impulse to turn back. Instantly, she realized that she had no choice. She had to help Nicholas. He had become an indelible part of her. To go on living with the knowledge that she'd simply left him in peril would fill her with more guilt than any crime she'd ever committed.

Quickly, she left the cave and searched the area. Farther along the shore, several tall shrubs were clustered together. Taking Elaina by the shoulders, she said to her sister,

"Listen to me. I need you to hide behind those plants."

"Why?" Elaina protested. "We have to get out of here."

"We will, but there's something I have to do first. I need you to be brave, okay?"

Elaina nodded. "You won't be long, will you?"

Feigning a smile, she shook her head. "I won't. Just wait for me."

Her sister agreed and scampered off toward the shrubs. Daniela waited until Elaina was safely hidden before she turned back toward the cave. She didn't know how long she would be or what would transpire once she returned. She drew out the gun Nicholas had slipped into her pocket. The man she loved was inside, and she wasn't leaving without him.

Chapter 19

Nicholas ripped the heavy wooden stake from the ground and swung it at the warlock just as he came at him. The man was knocked off his feet, but was resilient. He came at him again.

Another crash resounded about the room as Simion managed to topple a second gargoyle statue. On the ground, Stefan fought vigorously, while the screeching of the souls rose above the chaos. The ribbon-like coils of light began to drift toward the remaining statues. However, the chanting of the witch had ceased for Nicholas no longer remained in the circle of the host.

"Keep chanting!" Andrew screamed.

The Raba witch who stood before the book looked uneasy. "But there is no host," she protested.

"I don't care. I want my soul in Gabriel's body. Read it," he insisted.

Another statue was pushed to the ground and it shattered to pieces.

Magdelene stepped forward. "The spell was not written that way, Andrew. It must be followed in sequence."

Andrew reached into his cloak and pulled a gun out. "It's too late for sequence. I said keep chanting!" He pointed the gun at her, his eyes blazing with anger.

Magdelene looked to the witch and nodded. And so the chanting began again.

Nicholas laid a fist into the jaw of the warlock, rendering him unconscious. He turned his attention toward the platform just in time to see the souls of the gargoyles pass into the stone. In anguish, he watched as cracks began to snake up their legs. It was too late. They'd failed in their mission. He drew the dagger that Adela had given him. It could be used only once. He would save it for Gabriel.

He would've headed for the statue of Gabriel, but he was halted as shots rang out and one of the statues broke away into pieces. He found the source and was immediately filled with both rage and admiration.

Daniela stood in the doorway, his gun held firmly in her hands. She aimed for the next statue and destroyed it without flinching.

"Stop her!" Andrew shouted.

The Raba witch who'd broken the runes raced toward Daniela. However, her steps faltered as the room began to tremble. Deep and mournful wailings arose as all of the souls were pulled from their hosts. The incantation, improperly performed, was forcing them toward the statue of Gabriel.

Stalactites were shaken from the ceiling and fell to skewer two of the warlocks. The witch continued her chanting and even the souls of these fallen men were summoned and commanded toward Gabriel's form.

Nicholas dived out of the way, avoiding a sharp stalactite and certain death. A glance across the room revealed Daniela running toward him. Skillfully, she dodged the falling projectiles. Andrew's men and the Raba warlocks allowed her free passage as she was no longer of any concern to them. They were retreating from the room that was fast collapsing. Simion and Stefan had moved off to the side of the room, but stood their ground.

A huge stalactite came cascading down above the altar where the witch stood chanting. She glanced up and slammed the spell book shut, stepping back just before the altar was completely destroyed. The force of it knocked her to the ground and the book skidded somewhere off to the side.

At that moment, Andrew's screams joined the confusion. His face was contorted in agony and he gripped his chest. His knees buckled and he collapsed to the ground. The symbol about him began to glow. And soon so did the one that had been drawn about Gabriel.

Daniela appeared at Nicholas's side. She quickly looked him over.

"Are you okay?" she was gasping for breath.

He pulled her to him, embracing her tightly. "We are too late. I will have only one chance at attempting to reverse the spell."

A cry echoed across the room. "No! Get up!"

Their attention snapped to the Raba witch who was racing toward her sister. Her twin remained on the ground near the pile of rubble that had once been the altar. Around her, the circle of the host glowed brightly.

A second later, her body jerked into an arch and her eyes flew open. Her mouth opened, and with her scream a ray of light was emitted. Simultaneously, Andrew's cry echoed again and his soul slipped from his lifeless body.

The Raba witch gripped her sister's body and

dragged her from the circle. She cradled her in her arms and sobbed.

Magdelene inched around Gabriel's statue. "Quick, girl, retrieve the Book of Spirits!"

Simion, who'd come to stand near Nicholas, reached down and picked up the book. He sent Magdelene a challenging look. If she wanted the book, she'd have to come and retrieve it herself.

Magdelene paused in her advance and behind her, a narrow gateway opened. Casting Simion a venomous look, she stepped into it and disappeared.

"Mother!" the remaining Raba witch cried out just as the portal snapped shut.

Stefan moved to apprehend her, but Simion placed a hand on his arm. "Leave her be. She has suffered enough."

They turned and watched as the two new souls joined the others in the statue of Gabriel. The trembling of the room ceased and silence ensued. Nicholas set Daniela aside and his grip flexed on the dagger. Simion and Stefan had come to stand at his side and together they waited.

The awakening began with the subtle sound of stone cracking. It started at the base of the statue and snaked its way up along the thick legs, moving higher still. Stone began to break away and flesh formed beneath the outer layer.

Gabriel was the same in face and form, but he wasn't as Nicholas remembered him. His eyes shifted with apparent madness and his body flinched. It seemed that the souls within him were engaged in a battle for supremacy. And when he cried out, it was with the voices of many. He tossed his head and leapt into the air.

Nicholas pursued. This abomination couldn't be allowed out into the world. Gabriel spun about with a speed that was even unnatural for the greatest of gargoyle warriors. Nicholas deduced that more than just the souls of the Raba warlocks had been forced into the host, their abilities had melded, as well.

Gabriel slipped through the hole in the cave

roof and out into the night. Nicholas quickly exited the cave and watched as the large form began to make its way across the lake. He knew that he would never catch him. Thinking fast, he aimed the dagger and propelled it toward his target.

Gabriel cried out as the blade penetrated the flesh of his back. Immediately the dagger incinerated in a burst of light. It had done nothing. The powerful beating of Gabriel's wings filled the quiet of the night as he continued making his way across the expanse of water.

Nicholas released a shuddering breath and his head fell. It had been too much to hope that Adela's spell would've been effective against such a large entity. His fear was great for now the world would have to stand against the terrible beast.

He dragged his attention back to the figure of his uncle. Oddly, Gabriel had paused above the center of the lake. His body jerked and it seemed he suffered great agony. Before

Nicholas could guess what was afoot, Gabriel's movements froze and even from that distance, he could make out the cold stone that quickly consumed him.

The spell had worked.

Gabriel's final cry died on the wind as his body, now stone, toppled from the air and landed in the water with a colossal splash.

Nicholas looked out over the river. The morning fog hung low, but was not enough to obscure the many boats and divers that littered the water.

After the reverse spell had taken effect, they'd all returned to the estate to inform his parents of what had taken place. Lord Victor had been devastated to learn that Andrew, his trusted friend and cousin, had turned out to be the traitor and had faced his death as a result. It had destroyed him even more to hear of Gabriel's unfortunate end.

Even now, as Lord Victor stood in silence,

his face was ashen. The situation had intensified even more, now that after three hours of
combing the lake, the statue or even remnants
of it had yet to be found.

Nicholas sighed and headed back to the car.
It wasn't determined if they had cause to be
concerned or not, for the lake was as wide as
it was deep. A statue, even of that magnitude,
could've been carted away on a strong current
as it sunk to the bottom.

Daniela stood against the car. She was wrapped in a wool blanket and she looked exhausted.
She smiled wanly as he approached. He'd insisted that she remain at the estate with Elaina,
but she'd been unwilling to leave his side; at
least not until all matters had been resolved. His
mother had been surprised to learn Daniela's
true identity, but he'd not been abashed in telling her that he'd found the woman he wanted
to be with.

"They haven't found the statue yet?" she asked.
He shook his head and pulled her into his

arms. Carefully, he studied her face. In just a short time, she'd come to mean so much to him. She'd placed her life on the line and braved unimaginable adversities to assure his safety. He wanted her in his life. He needed her, but she couldn't go on living the way she had been.

"What will you do when you return to New York?" he asked quietly.

She looked away and sighed. He understood that she'd continued stealing because it was the only way she knew how to provide for herself and her sister. Inside, she was an honest and caring woman whose only crime had been being born into a less than fortunate situation. And he wanted to help her.

"If you are willing to give up stealing—" he took hold of her chin and forced her to meet his eyes "—I may have need for someone with your expertise in handling and caring for antiques."

A slow smile curved her lips and her eyes began to shimmer. "Why would you do that for me, Nicholas? After all the trouble I've caused you and your family?"

A serious look crossed his face as his head dipped and their lips brushed. "Because I love you," he breathed.

Her gasp was drowned as his mouth claimed her for a fierce kiss.

* * * * *